THE LUMP IN THE MIDDLE

C.S. ADLER has written some of her published books for children and young adults in Wellfleet, Massachusetts, where she spends her summers walking the beaches and working the computer. The rest of her novels are written in Niskayuna, a town next to Schenectady, New York. At one time Carole Adler taught English in middle school in Niskayuna, and she and her husband raised their three sons there.

Many of Adler's books have also been published in Japan, Germany, England, Denmark, and Austria. She won the Golden Kite Award and the William Allen White Award for her first book, *The Magic of the Glits,* and has since won other literary prizes. Her books have often been on the Children's Choices list and have been chosen for many state lists.

THE LUMP in THE MIDDLE

C.S. ADLER

AN AVON CAMELOT BOOK

Acknowledgments:

*With gratitude to Chris Richardson
who suggested this book be written,
and thanks to Maureen
for her insight into the problem
of being a middle child.*

AVON BOOKS
A division of
The Hearst Corporation
1350 Avenue of the Americas
New York, New York 10019

Text copyright © 1989 by C.S. Adler
Published by arrangement with Clarion Books, Houghton Mifflin Company
Library of Congress Catalog Card Number: 88-35922
ISBN: 0-380-71176-1
RL: 5.6

First Avon Camelot Printing: December 1991

CAMELOT TRADEMARK REG. U.S. PAT. OFF. AND IN OTHER COUNTRIES, MARCA REGISTRADA, HECHO EN U.S.A.

Printed in the U.S.A.

OPM 10 9 8 7 6 5 4 3

To Stephanie Tolan,
with admiration for her talent
as a writer and as a critic

Kelsey lay awake in the dark of the tiny bedroom listening to the rain. It had been rushing down for three days, and was still pounding on the roof and smacking at the windows of the summer cottage with frightening energy. Carefully, so as not to wake her sister Ria, who was sleeping three feet away, Kelsey felt for the cold cylinder of the flashlight and the soft square of her notepaper on the night table. Making a cave of her blanket, she bent cross-legged under it and began writing another letter to her friend Jennifer.

"You know how you always say you can learn from bad experiences?" she wrote with the flashlight clenched under her jaw. "Well, after three days of being cooped up with my family I learned why I don't get along with them. I AM A LUMP IN THEIR MIDDLE. I am, Jennifer. Really. I don't fit, and they'd all like to get rid of me, even Ria and Dad. Not that I blame them. You think I'm nice and that everybody likes me, but that's with my friends. With my family, I turn mean. I do, Jennifer. I say awful things and fight all the time. I'll turn into a monster with just them around this summer. Won't you please, please come and be with me?"

Kelsey's hot blood cooled slowly as she listened to the quarreling rain. Jennifer had already told her she couldn't come. The trip was too long and too expensive and Jennifer needed the money she was earning baby-sitting. Sighing, Kelsey flicked off the flashlight, stowed it under the bed with the notepaper, and returned to the task of falling asleep.

The next she knew, Ria was standing beside her, dressed as if she were ready for a match, in tennis shorts and a T-shirt. Ria was always ready for tennis. It was her only passion.

"Everybody's eaten," Ria said. "Mom wants to know if she should save you some pancake batter."

"No, thanks. I'm not getting up until the rain stops," Kelsey said.

Ria nudged her. "Come on. We can play Scrabble. I'm only two games ahead of you."

"Scrabble!" Kelsey groaned with disgust and pulled her pillow over her face. Ria tugged it off.

"Monopoly then?"

Kelsey studied her fifteen-year-old sister's face. Ria, Maria, looked like a long-nosed angel with her straight blond hair, serene expression, and the extra-long eyelashes they all had. "Don't you hate it that you're not at tennis camp, Ria?"

"It might be raining there, too."

"But at least you'd be with kids your own age instead of stuck here with your boring family."

"Speak for yourself, Kelsey," Ria said. "I'll tell Dad he can eat the rest of the pancakes, then."

Ria left and Kelsey lay staring at the old-fashioned acoustic tile ceiling, thinking about her father. Before Sara was born, when Kelsey was Daddy's girl, she'd sat on his lap and ridden the roaring lawn mower like a wild chariot while he drove. Back and forth they'd charged, as the green grass fell and the blue sky smiled and she gripped the railings of his strong arms. Her daddy's arms. Then Sara was born and six-year-old Kelsey was told to stop acting like a baby. Not by Dad. But still, she'd had to stand outside and watch Sara, cute, homely Sara with her big brown laughing eyes, cuddling up to him.

"You blame Sara," Ria always said. "But it's your own fault."

Sometimes it was. Kelsey still squirmed with shame when she thought of how she'd acted this spring when Dad came home and told them he'd lost his job. At first, he'd looked so wounded that she'd thrown her arms around his neck and crooned, "It'll be all right, Daddy. Don't feel bad. It'll be all right." Fine. But later, when it turned out they'd have to sell the house and leave Cincinnati forever — meaning she would lose all her friends — she'd been horrified. How could she live without her friends?

"I guess most high schools have a tennis team," Ria had said bravely. And even little Sara had been flip. "I didn't want my same teacher again next year anyway." Kelsey, only Kelsey, had burst into tears and screamed at him, "You can't do this to me!"

"Don't be so selfish, Kelsey," Mom had said and whispered to hush her. "Your father feels bad enough. Stop it now."

Gulping down her tears, Kelsey had apologized. "I'm sorry. I'm sorry, Daddy." But oh, how his eyes had clouded with grief, with a hurt she could never fix. She'd cursed herself for not being like Ria who kept it all in and cried quietly in her bed at night so that Dad wouldn't know how much it meant to her to give up her tennis team and her chance of becoming its top-ranked player.

Kelsey shuddered. If only the rain would stop . . . if only she could be someone else. She reached for the notepaper under the bed and reread her letter to Jennifer. Yes, it was true. Her friends liked her and her family didn't. And even being in Cape Cod wasn't going to help.

They were here because their house had sold too fast; so Aunt Syl had offered them her cottage in Wellfleet. "I know one young beach lover who'll be glad," Aunt Syl had written. She'd meant Kelsey. But what good was a bay beach only a few hundred feet across the road when rain was pattering onto the roof and plinking on the windows and seeping into the basement? Unless the rain could be ignored.

Abruptly Kelsey flung aside her covers. She pulled her swimsuit from a dresser drawer built into the knotty pine wall, getting goosebumps on her slim, freckled arms from the chilly air as she stripped to put it on. Wearing the hooded green sweatshirt that came midway down her thighs took care of the goose-bumps. Mom had bought the sweatshirt, of course. She always bought Kelsey things in green or blue to go with her red hair. Kelsey chose pink or red or black when she picked her own clothes. Then she'd come home and have a fight with Mother about clashing colors and end up feeling so ugly that she'd hate the new thing before she ever wore it.

It was so late that everybody had finished with the bathroom. Kelsey took her time, then went to the kitchen to scrounge up some breakfast.

Mom was scrubbing away at the metal rims of the burners on Aunt Syl's old stove.

"Why are you fussing with those, Mom?" Kelsey said pleasantly. "You know Aunt Syl won't care if they're clean or not."

"I intend to leave this place spotless," Mother said. "It's the least I can do to repay her."

"She might get insulted if it's cleaner than she keeps it. Like you're saying she's a bad housekeeper or something."

"She *is* a bad housekeeper. And I'm a good one," Mom said. She was a square, practical woman, good at whatever she did. She could make even the rowdiest of her seventh-grade math students behave.

Kelsey poured herself a glass of milk and drank it while trying to see out the tear-streaked windows. "Where're Ria and Dad?" she asked.

"In the basement sopping up water," her mother said. "It's coming in over the sills."

"And *I'm* helping Mommy." Sara's voice came from somewhere in the living room. As usual, she sounded pleased with herself.

"Sara's getting those spiderwebs off the chair bottoms," Mom said.

Kelsey stepped to where she could look over the countertop into the living room – their eating, playing, reading, and TV-watching space. Sara was crouched under the wooden table swiping at chair legs with a white cloth.

"Seen any spiders yet, Sara?" Kelsey asked.

"Just one." Sara sounded as casual as if she'd never been terrified of spiders.

"I hope it wasn't Charlotte," Kelsey said.

"Charlotte?" Sara repeated, her eyes widening.

"You know, the spider in that book I read you." It had been *Charlotte's Web* that cured Sara of her fear of spiders.

Sara crawled out from under the table and announced, "I'm not going to dust anymore, Mommy."

"Sure you are," Mom said, unaware of whom she was up against in spiders. "Kelsey, how about you helping too?"

"I will when I come back from the beach."

"The *beach*?" Mother frowned. "Are you crazy? You can't go to the beach in this weather."

"Yes, I can." It had to be better than being cooped up with the family.

"Yesterday you wouldn't go out in the rain to shop with us, but today you're going to the beach in a deluge?" Mother sounded incredulous.

"*I* went shopping and Daddy bought me something," Sara crowed.

Kelsey gritted her teeth. Was Sara really so obnoxious, or was she, Kelsey, still jealous of a baby sister who got all the attention? Whichever, they'd be fighting in a minute if Kelsey didn't make a fast exit. Then the parents would blame her. They always did when Sara was involved.

Pulling on the slicker that had hung on the peg behind the front door, Kelsey started out barefoot. Sneakers would be warmer, but once they were wet, they'd never dry in this weather. She mushed across the slick, pine-needled driveway onto the sand road, hoping that the tide would be low enough so that she could walk along the beach. High tide brought the bay right up to the retaining walls people had built to protect their cottages from storm-driven water.

It was almost high tide. Only a narrow strip of sand remained in front of the concrete retaining wall to the left.

Kelsey looked to the right, through streamers of rain, toward the long rock jetty that marked the entrance to Wellfleet Harbor. A light at its tip helped boats navigate in the channel, but nobody, not even a fisherman, was out there today. The bay looked desolate. It would be like death to walk into that steely water. She'd planned to swim every day no matter what the weather, but this was too grim. Would they miss her if she drowned? Ria would. Sara would be glad. Mother might be too, although she'd never admit it.

So Sara had gone off to shop with the parents yesterday. Big deal. Sara liked having them all to herself. The only reason Kelsey hadn't gone was Dad had said he was also stopping at the hardware store, and Mom had admitted she planned to check out a few more craft shops. Sara loved craft and gift shops, especially ones that sold junk. She was an acquisitive kid with lots of collections — dolls, of course, and shells and stones and stickers and colored glass bottles and turtles, especially turtles. And sure enough, the parents had bought her another turtle. They'd had to sell the big house in Cincinnati because the mortgage payments were too much to handle on just Mom's salary, but Sara's millionth turtle, *that* they could afford.

What galled Kelsey most was that Mom had acted as if Kelsey were outrageous when she'd mentioned she could use a new pair of shorts, even though the shorts were on sale and didn't cost much — the budget, you know. "You'll just have to make do this summer," Mom had said. No wonder Kelsey envied cute, goody, seven-year-old Sara sometimes. Being thirteen and awkward, with hideous brown freckles and hair the color of rusty nails and a mother who hated her, was so depressing.

The rain cooled Kelsey's anger. A red sailboat bobbed on its mooring, bright against the drabness of veiled bay and sky. The pearly white inside of an oyster shell caught her eye, and she picked it up to add to the collection on the deck. At the end of the summer they'd have to sort through hundreds of shells to come up with the shoeboxful worth taking home. If they had a home. If they didn't, maybe they'd go back to Cincinnati. Mother could keep her teaching job, and they could find a little house to rent near their old big one. . . .

"It could take a year to find a job, the right kind of job," Dad had warned them during the belt-tightening family discussion. He'd been a manager of engineering for a small company. That was when they'd all solemnly promised not to even want anything nonessential that cost money. It was no problem for Ria. Her only wish was for the expensive white ceramic tennis racquet which she'd been lucky enough to get for her fifteenth birthday just before Dad's company folded. No problem for Sara, because budgets didn't affect what she got. Kelsey was the one who had to economize. Like not letting her call her friends, not at all, not even once a week on Sundays — except one person for five minutes. Five minutes a week when she was addicted to five hours a day! That was like condemning her to solitary confinement.

This very minute while she stood there with her feet chilling in the wet sand and the rain dripping off her eyelashes, her friends were gathered at the swimming pool: Jennifer and Cathy and boys too probably. "Lucky Kelsey," they'd be saying, "on the beach in Cape Cod."

Resolutely, Kelsey set off down the narrow strip of beach to the left. She'd said she was going for a walk and she would. Maybe she'd find something wonderful, like a baby seal. The newspaper had talked about baby seals being found on beaches somewhere on the Cape. If she couldn't have Jennifer, a baby seal would be nice.

What would really be a miracle to find would be a kid her own age, maybe somebody from one of the cottages that lined the low dunes overlooking the bay. Those cottages had a view of the sunset. Kelsey would escape from her family and spend her evenings sunset-watching with her friend. Yes. And suppose the friend was a boy instead of a girl, a boy who liked redheaded girls with skinny legs.

She remembered how buck-toothed Lenny Markowitz had tried to kiss her at the seventh-grade party. She'd ducked and he'd licked her ear. Oh, how gross that had been! Maybe a girl would be better. She could talk to a girl and not worry about whether her hair was frizzing.

Kelsey sighed. Who was she kidding? She'd never meet anyone in this rain. Her feet felt cramped from the cold. She might as well go back and earn goody points dusting spiderwebs.

Their car was gone when she reached the plain gray-shingled cottage. Good, she thought. Maybe she wouldn't have to dust spiderwebs after all. She'd make herself hot cocoa and warm her feet and read.

The first person she saw in the living room was Mom, curled up on the couch with a crossword puzzle. Dad must have gone somewhere alone in the car, because there was Ria – Ria the traitor – sitting at the table playing Scrabble with Sara.

"What are you doing?" Kelsey screamed.

Everyone looked up at her startled. "Nothing," Mom said.

"You're playing Scrabble with Sara," Kelsey accused Ria.

"You didn't want to play with me and Sara wanted to learn," Ria defended herself. But Kelsey knew that Ria understood what it meant that she be Ria's Scrabble partner. Ria had taught her to play. Kelsey could still remember how proud she'd felt the day she finally got good enough to be a challenge to her big sister.

"I like Scrabble," Sara said happily. "It's easy. You always said it was too hard for me, Kelsey, but it's easy."

"Why don't you go play with your turtles?" Kelsey snapped. She couldn't bear it that the baby was stealing Ria from her. But mentioning turtles had been a mistake.

Tears filled Sara's brown-dolly eyes. She'd had to leave most of her beloved collection of turtles in storage when they moved out of their big house in Cincinnati. All she had here, besides the new turtle, were a few miniatures and First Turtle. First Turtle was the cushion Mom had made her from green quilting with soft yellow satin for the belly, legs, and head. First Turtle had started Sara's fixation with the ugly, snaky-headed creatures.

"Kelsey, *why* do you have to be mean?" Mom smacked down her pen. "Ria was just trying to entertain Sara, which is more than you've done the past three days."

"How can you say that? I did the jigsaw puzzle, didn't I?" The first day it rained Mom had found a thousand-piece jigsaw puzzle in Aunt Syl's utility closet, and the whole family had worked on it without much bickering. Fun, until Mom had to point out how pleasant it was to have everybody so congenial.

"You spent the entire day playing Scrabble with Ria yesterday," Mom said, "and today – "

"Always me!" Kelsey cried. "It's always me who's bad. And I haven't *done* anything!" She raced to her room, slid under the covers and pulled them over her head. Her feet were chilled; her stomach was empty – she'd only had a glass of milk for breakfast – and it was early July. Two whole months of awful, dreadful family togetherness remained in what was bound to be the worst summer of her life.

2

Kelsey opened her eyes to blue. Outside the bedroom window, behind the spiky pine needles, shone a spectacular blue sky. "Wake up, Ria. It's a beach day," she shouted.

Ria scooched more deeply into her pillow and mumbled, "G'way," when Kelsey tickled her bare arm with a feather from a leaky pillow. Except for tennis, Ria resisted awakening in the morning. In fact, unless she'd had a hard time sleeping, Kelsey was the only early riser in the family. She'd been a hyperactive baby who never slept, Mom claimed. Kelsey considered that another put-down, another way of calling her a difficult kid.

Not a single T-shirt remained in her drawer. Mom had said she wasn't doing any wash until the rain stopped and she could dry it on the line outside. Kelsey had clean underpants and bras only because she'd washed them by hand and hung them over the shower rod to dry. Wearing soiled clothes disgusted her.

Quietly she sneaked open Ria's drawer. Ria owned lots of T-shirts because she needed them for tennis. Kelsey eyed her sleeping sister and decided it was

Ria's own fault that she wasn't awake so that Kelsey could ask to borrow one of her three remaining clean tees. If Ria were awake, she'd say yes — eventually.

Kelsey's hand hovered over the embroidered blue shirt that Ria saved for special occasions, hesitated on the tee she'd won at a tennis tournament, and closed on the oversized shirt Ria had bought herself with baby-sitting money. It was brand-new, pale blue and long sleeved. It came halfway down Kelsey's thighs and felt good in the cool of early morning. She'd be careful with it, and wash it out by hand tonight to make it good as new for Ria. She would; she really would.

Dad was writing at the breakfast table. Kelsey set her glass of milk down next to his coffee and sat beside him, opposite Mom and Sara. "We'll go to an ocean beach this morning, won't we?" Kelsey said.

"Maybe later," Dad muttered. He was drafting another of the dozens of letters he'd been sending out about job opportunities.

"I guess I'll go to the bay meanwhile," she said.

"How about taking Sara with you," Mom suggested between bites of toast.

"You said I could bake cookies, Mommy," Sara said. She was molding a turtle from clay. They'd found it in the utility closet, along with such items as the puzzle, cards, and an ancient Monopoly game, all of which Aunt Syl had probably collected for her renters.

"Don't you want to go to the beach?" Mom asked Sara in surprise.

"It's too cold now." Sara was wearing shorts and a sweater. "I'd rather make cookies."

Mom nodded. "Okay, plain sugar cookies. Maybe your sister will help you. Hmm, Kelsey?"

"But early morning is the best time to find birds and stuff on the beach," Kelsey said quickly.

"What's another word for opportunity," Dad asked. He'd crossed out as much as he'd written.

"Chance," Kelsey told him, "opening, challenge."

"Challenge, that's it, thanks." Dad wrote another line.

"Dad, did you write to that guy who was always saying you ought to go to work for his company?" Kelsey suddenly thought to ask.

"You mean Masden, the competition? He wouldn't want me now, honey. Nobody wants a guy who's been fired."

"You weren't fired," Mom said. "It wasn't your fault the president ran the business into the ground."

Dad shook his head and hunched into himself. It was a sore subject.

"Maybe Kelsey's right," Mom said. "You ought to ask Masden if — "

"Lay off, will you, please." Dad was tight-lipped.

They all visibly drew back from him.

"It wouldn't hurt you to bake cookies with Sara, Kelsey," Mom said then, "and it would help me. I've got all that wash to do."

"But the *sun's* out," Kelsey objected. "It's stupid to bake cookies when the sun's out."

"I'm *not* stupid." Sara said indignantly.

"I didn't say you were. I just said — "

"All right, all right, forget it." Mother threw her hands up in defeat. "Everybody can go do what they want, including me. Let the wash wait."

"I'll put a load in before I go," Kelsey offered.

Mom hesitated, then admitted, "That would help."

"I can't find my new shirt," Ria said from behind Kelsey. "It's not in my drawer." Kelsey slid down in her chair, but it was too late. "Kelsey!" Ria pounced. "You promised you'd stop borrowing my stuff without asking me."

"You wouldn't wake up. So how could I ask?"

"Take it off."

"I don't have anything to wear."

"Tough." Ria folded her arms forbiddingly.

"But Ria, you've got three clean tees," Kelsey pointed out. She turned to her mother. "Mine are all in the wash, Mom. You always say sisters should share."

"You should have asked her permission," Mom said.

"Why can't you ever, ever, *ever* take my side!" Kelsey cried.

"I don't have any clean shirts either," Sara said. "So I wore a sweater. And when it's hot, I'll put on my bathing suit."

"Oh, shut up," Kelsey said.

"Kelsey, you don't have to be nasty to Sara," Mom said.

Dad smacked the table with his hand so hard the

dishes bounced. "Would you all squabble someplace else? This is an important letter I'm drafting."

"Here, take your stupid T-shirt," Kelsey said. She was pulling it off over her head when she remembered she was wearing underwear, not a swimsuit. She yanked the shirt back down, knocking over a jar of raspberry preserves which splattered over Ria's precious new shirt.

Ria yelped. "Kelsey, you did that on purpose!"

"I did not."

"You ruined it."

"I'll wash it, Ria. I'll wash it right now." It alarmed Kelsey to upset her even-tempered sister. Even at match point, Ria never lost her cool, but there she stood, fighting back tears. All at once, Kelsey realized what was wrong. Not the T-shirt so much as everything else – missing out on tennis camp, the effort to be extra good for Dad's sake, the strain of all the cooped-up rainy days. "I'm sorry, Ria," Kelsey said with sympathy. "Really, I am."

"Go to the beach," Mother told her, as if she thought getting rid of Kelsey would improve everyone's temper. "I'll throw the shirt in the wash. Don't worry, Ria, it'll be good as new by tomorrow."

Feeling miserable, Kelsey ran to her room. She put on her old swimsuit. Her chest, which had gotten bigger than Ria's all of a sudden, swelled over the top of the suit embarrassingly this year, but it would have to do. She rinsed Ria's T-shirt in the sink, flung a towel over her shoulders, and fled the house. They didn't want her around. None of them wanted her, not even Ria who was usually on her side.

Running calmed her. She flew along the road to the beach entrance and kept going. It was easier running on the hard clam flats, now exposed by low tide, but the air was chilly for July. The water splashing her bare feet felt warmer than the air. The only people on the beach were a pair near the jetty getting a Windsurfer ready to sail. The gaudy orange and green and yellow and red sail was the most colorful object in sight. Kelsey ran toward it, scattering a platoon of sturdy herring gulls on the way. They rose on arched silver wings, wheeled over the water, and resettled on the beach behind her.

A bony-faced boy, who looked about Ria's age, was squatting beside the Windsurfer. A man in long pants and a windbreaker sat in a beach chair next to him. They both had long, sharp jaws and high cheekbones with deep-set eyes. Father and son, Kelsey guessed.

"Hi," she directed her greeting between the two. "It's sort of cold to sail without a wet suit, isn't it?"

The boy looked up and then down quickly. He had an interesting face, easy to sketch, but it was the man who answered her. "Gabe's been itching to try wind-surfing ever since we got here. Let's hope that water's warmer than it looks."

"Did you rent it?" Kelsey asked of the Windsurfer.

When the boy didn't answer, the man said, "Right at the town dock. You a windsurfing aficionado?"

"No, I just like to watch."

"I'm with you," the man said, "but a chance to get dumped in the drink was what Gabe wanted for his birthday. No accounting for tastes, is there?" He had a mischievous smile. His face was broader than his son's, more open. Kelsey smiled back at him.

"It'll be warmer this afternoon," she said.

"Me, I'd wait, or go back and see about a wet suit," the man said, "but Gabe's a real he-man."

"Dad! Don't mock me," Gabe said. He glanced up at Kelsey then struggled to tighten the sail some more with his bare toes propped against the mast. "My father's a joker," he said.

"You live around here?" the father asked Kelsey.

"Well, for the summer. My aunt lent us her cottage because my father — because we had to sell our house in Cincinnati."

"And they're slugabeds, all except you, right?" He was inviting information.

"No, they're up, but not ready to go beaching yet. I couldn't wait. Wasn't the rain awful?"

"Totally unfair for it to rain like that on vacation."

"Totally." Kelsey agreed. "Are you staying nearby?"

"Yep, we're renting a shack a ways back. No rich relatives with cottages, unfortunately."

"Oh, Aunt Syl's not rich," Kelsey said. "She just got the cottage as a divorce settlement from her first husband. Mostly she rents it out, but this summer it was too late for renting by the time she found out she couldn't use it. She's a journalist and she got a job writing about paradors in Spain, and my dad's her favorite brother so — " Kelsey stopped to take a breath and was embarrassed to realize that she'd blurted out private family business like a little kid. "I'm a beach nut," she said to change the subject.

"So's Gabe," the man said. "You ever try windsurfing?"

She shook her head. "It looks like you have to be pretty strong to handle it, and I'm not very muscular."

"Well built, but definitely not muscular," the man said.

The remark made Kelsey tingle pleasantly, even though she crossed her arms over her chest. But Gabe scolded, "Hey, Dad, cool it, will you?"

"What'd I say? Ladies like compliments, honest ones. Don't they?" he asked Kelsey.

Before she could agree, Gabe said, "She's a girl, not a lady."

"What do you mean telling this pretty girl she's not a lady," his father shot back. "And you're giving *me* lessons in tact?"

Kelsey laughed, and even Gabe unbent enough to smile. Having tightened the sheet on the sail to his satisfaction, the boy tucked in the excess line and stood up. He was tall, built slim and strong like a runner or a tennis player; but he seemed to be ignoring her. Maybe he just didn't find her interesting, Kelsey thought.

"I'm Herb Altman and this is my son, Gabe," the man said, holding his hand out.

She shook it briefly. "I'm Kelsey Morris."

"Well, Miss Morris, my apologies if I've embarrassed you," Herb said. "I was just trying to be friendly in my own bumbling way."

"I know," she said and caught herself quickly. "I mean, you're not bumbling."

"I guess I'm ready," Gabe said.

"Want help getting it to the water?" she asked.

"No, thanks. I can manage." His lips perked up at either end in something near a smile. "You don't have to listen to Herb. He'll talk your ear off if you let him. He does a radio talk show. Talking's his business."

"Thanks a bunch, Gabe," Herb Altman said lightly. "Nothing like a put-down from your own son to take the wind out of a man's sails." He stayed in his chair while Gabe dragged the Windsurfer into the water.

"Do you really have your own talk show?" Kelsey asked.

"Small station, small show." Now that his son was out of earshot, there was a down note in his voice that hadn't been there before.

"But that's such a wonderful job," she said. "I mean, I never met anyone on radio before."

"It's a job, like any other. You get used to it."

Sensing that he didn't want to talk about it, she hesitated. Should she say good-bye and leave even though she didn't want to go yet? She looked at Gabe who was standing on the Windsurfer in the shallows, reaching for the sail which lay on the water, open and ready.

"Don't expect too flashy a performance," Herb said quietly. "He's only had one lesson. This is his first time out on his own."

Just then Gabe grasped the sail and heaved it upright. She was impressed. "He looks as if he knows what he's doing. He must be very athletic."

"He does okay. Good runner. Not on a team yet, but he's only a sophomore. Next year, who knows." Herb sounded comfortable again now that he was talking about his son. Kelsey gave him credit for being too modest to like talking about himself.

"My sister's a tennis champ," she said. "I mean, she's really good. All I can do is swim a little."

"Older sister or younger?" Herb asked.

She opened her mouth, then shut it while she considered. If Gabe was a sophomore, he was fifteen or sixteen. Saying that her fifteen-year-old sister was older than she would give her age away. Gabe would certainly ignore her if he knew she was only thirteen. "Ria and I are about the same age," Kelsey said. "Very close. I have a younger sister, Sara, who's only seven."

"You in high school?" Herb asked.

"Hmmm?" she stalled.

"Well, don't be insulted. You could be one of these amazingly young-looking matrons with kids of your own for all I know. Guessing a woman's age is beyond me."

"I'm fifteen," she heard herself say. "That is, I'm going to be a sophomore this fall." The lie had flown out of her mouth, taking her breath with it.

Gabe, who'd looked so expert, suddenly lost the sail and flopped off the board into waist-deep water. "Gusty near the shore," Herb said. His eyes had been on his son all the while he'd been talking to Kelsey. "Even the experts have a hard time occasionally."

"I should be getting back." Kelsey had an urgent need to run away from her lie. "My parents are probably wondering where I've gotten to. It was nice meeting you." She began backing away.

"Must you go?" Herb asked with a disappointment that turned to amusement as she continued rapidly backing away from him. "Well, see you around then," he said and waved. She waved back, turned, and raced off.

Gabe was on the board again, hauling the dripping sail out of the water, knees bent as if he were sitting on a chair. And there he went, off like a one-winged bird out past the jetty. Kelsey's heart pinged with longing. She'd never met a more attractive boy, and now if she saw him on the beach again, she wouldn't even dare say hello.

Not that it mattered. He hadn't liked her much. No wonder. She'd been so awkward. Why had she blurted out that stupid lie about her age? She could have avoided the question without saying exactly how old she was. She could have changed the subject. She could have said something clever. She'd die if they ever found out she was only thirteen.

She ran, hanging onto her towel. What would she do if she bumped into them on the beach when her *family* was with her? She could just imagine Mom saying, "No, it's Ria who's fifteen. Kelsey's only an immature thirteen year old." Humiliation.

Alone, she could talk to Gabe and his father, skirting her lie if she were careful. Or maybe she could take Ria into her confidence and get her to promise not to give Kelsey's age away. They could say they were twins. Ria wouldn't, though. Ria would never lie, and Sara was bound to show up and ruin things. What a fix she'd gotten herself in! Unless she kept her family away from the bay beach, she was bound to be found out. And he was so cute. Gabe, Gabriel. She quivered just thinking of his name.

Kelsey bounded up the steps onto the deck that encircled the cottage.

"There you are," Mom said. "We're all ready to go to Newcomb Hollow."

Newcomb Hollow was Dad's favorite ocean beach. "I'm ready too," Kelsey said. Clothes were flapping on the line in the sun, and Mom seemed to have forgotten her annoyance with Kelsey. In fact, Mom was looking cheerful. Good, now all Kelsey had to do was jump waves and figure a way out of the lie she'd told.

3

Kelsey stood on the cliff at the end of the beach parking lot, watching the bottle green waves below her swell until they burst and dissolved into a fizzy white foam edging for the beach. The narrow bed of warm, grainy sand, untouched by the sea, swooped up into the grass-topped dunes on which she stood. As always she was awed by the beauty of the ocean, by a sense of its endless living force, but today she seemed to be viewing it from outside a glass display case. If she spoke, she imagined her family wouldn't hear her. She was with them but apart.

Following the others down the steep path, she waited behind Ria and Sara for the parents to stake out territory with back rests and towels and bags. As soon as they'd settled near the lifeguard stand, Ria yelled, "Come on, Kelsey," and ran for the water.

She isn't mad at me anymore, Kelsey thought. Elated that Ria wasn't holding a grudge about the T-shirt, she dashed after her sister.

"Wait for me!" Sara squealed.

The display case shattered as Kelsey splashed into

the chill water. All at once she was there with her sisters. They jumped the waves and ducked the foaming breakers, hanging onto each other and screaming. They dodged the body surfers and the floats and the Styrofoam boards, tumbled in the surf and got scraped on stony patches until Sara said she'd had enough. Then they followed her out and snuggled into the yielding sand, mindless with pleasure.

"Aren't you going in the water, Dad?" Kelsey asked.

"I'm still thinking about it." He was leaning on his elbow just staring at the waves. Since he'd lost his job, he'd gotten too quiet, she thought. Silence had taken the place of his old authority.

"Want to build a sand castle then?" she asked, hoping to turn him on to one of his enthusiasms.

"You build one, honey, and I'll watch."

She shook her head. For her the main fun of sand turrets and roadways was seeing him become a little boy again when he was building them.

Ria was contemplating a young woman as blond and sinewy as herself perched on a lifeguard's stand. "I wonder what you'd need to get a lifeguard's job here," she murmured.

"I thought you were going to be a tennis pro," Mom said over the top of the novel she was reading. Disguised by straw hat, glasses, and loose beach robe, Mom was barely recognizable there in her beach chair.

"I'm not good enough to become a pro," Ria said.

"You have to start practically when you're born, or forget it."

"Of course you're good enough," Mom assured her. "You can do anything you want."

"You didn't tell *me* that when I said I wanted to be an astronaut," Kelsey couldn't resist pointing out.

"Kelsey, for heaven's sake, that was last winter!" Mom said.

"But you laughed," Kelsey insisted. She'd done a report on Sally Ride, and her mother's reaction to her enthusiasm for the astronaut had devastated Kelsey.

"I laughed because it was ridiculous. Astronauts excel in math and science. All you excel at is being difficult."

"Hey," Dad protested. "We're at the beach, remember? No fighting."

"I can excel," Kelsey muttered. She buried her face in her arms. Mother considered her a poor student just because she had gotten a few "C"s in math for neglecting homework assignments. She'd explained that she'd understood the concepts and had done well on tests, but Mom hadn't believed it.

Sara piped up suddenly, "I'm going to be a mother, like Mommy."

"Mom's a teacher," Ria said. "Being a mother's not a job. It's extra."

"And you don't get paid for it, even though it's hard work," Mother said.

"Fatherhood's hard too," Dad said. "And you don't get paid for that either, unfortunately."

"Well," Sara said, as if she were explaining something obvious, "that's just because children don't have any money."

They laughed, all except Kelsey who was outside the display case again. Sara could make them laugh. Why couldn't she? Discord seemed to be her contribution to the family, but with friends, she was the moderator. Look at how successful she'd been patching up the rift that occurred this past spring when Cathy mocked the way Jennifer dressed. "I can't help being poor!" Jennifer had cried pathetically to Kelsey who then had to spend hours talking Cathy into apologizing. If she could help her friends get along with each other, why couldn't she get along with her own family? Resisting her urge to cry, Kelsey sat up and asked Ria to go for a walk.

"Now?" Ria stretched her long arms.

"Please, Ria. I need you."

"Oh. Okay." Ria stood up.

"Can I come?" Sara asked.

"No," Kelsey said. "This is private."

"And anyway I need you to bury my legs in the sand, Sara," Dad said. "Would you do that for me?"

"Sure, Daddy," Sara said.

Kelsey gave her father a grateful smile.

As soon as they were out of earshot of the family, she told Ria, "I'm glad you're not still mad at me about the shirt. You're not, are you?"

"I only got mad because you promised you'd ask first."

It was true that Ria took promises seriously, but her

anger that morning had to have come from something deeper. "And besides you were feeling bad about not going to tennis camp, right?" Kelsey asked.

"I guess." Ria sighed. "I could play here if I could get to the courts and find someone to hit with."

Kelsey wondered if Gabe was good enough at tennis to play with Ria, but she didn't mention him. She wanted Gabe for herself. And Ria would be too much competition. Mom said Kelsey was selfish; well, maybe it was true. "Do you think I'm a rotten person, Ria?"

"No. You're normal." Ria was too used to Kelsey's questions to be fazed by them.

"Actually, I am sort of rotten. Not about the shirt, but – " she trailed off vaguely, "for other reasons."

"What have you done now?" Ria asked in a tone so like their mother's that Kelsey stopped wanting to confide in her. Ria was the only person available *to* confide in, though. Writing to friends meant an endless wait for a response that wouldn't even match her mood when it finally came.

"I met a boy on the beach this morning," Kelsey began.

"Really? Cute?"

"Uh huh. He probably doesn't like me though. Mostly I talked to his father."

"So?" Ria was interested.

Kelsey breathed deep of salt- and seaweed-scented air. "Well, so . . . Did you ever lie, Ria? Did you ever lie about anything?"

Ria considered. Water licked at their toes and

hissed away. They were tracing the wave edges like a pair of sandpipers. Ria took so much time to consider that Kelsey got annoyed. Had Ria asked *her* the question, she would have reassured her immediately, "Of course, I've lied."

"Not as far as I know," Ria said finally. "I mean, I can't remember lying about anything."

Kelsey dismissed that impatiently and argued, "But everybody tells white lies sometimes, Ria."

"You mean like saying that someone looks pretty when you don't think they do? . . . Yeah, I guess I may have done that."

"No, that's *not* what I mean . . . I lied about my age. I told Gabe's father I was fifteen, that you and I are about the same age."

"What'd you do that for?"

"Well, because I wanted Gabe to like me, and how could he like a kid who's two years younger than him?"

"You'd better tell the truth next time you see him. . . . Are you going to see him again?"

"I don't know." They were walking on smooth, colored stones left where waves had cut into a steep bank and swept out the sand. Here the high dunes were eroded down to ribs of reddish gray and brown clay. "It's not like I'm hurting anyone to lie about my age, Ria."

"But it's wrong. You'll get yourself in trouble."

"How? What's the big difference between thirteen and fifteen anyway?"

Ria looked at her reproachfully. Obviously, she saw a difference, but it wasn't her nature to argue. Instead, she said, "Well, don't expect me to cover for you if I happen to meet him."

"Oh, Ria!" Kelsey picked up a moon shell, but she dropped it when she saw the hole in its back. "You're getting to be as pluperfect proper as Mom. Lying about your age is no big deal." And she repeated, "It doesn't hurt anyone. Anyway, for all I know he could be leaving tomorrow."

"That'd be an easy out. I mean if he leaves," Ria said.

Suddenly Kelsey's concern about the lie was overwhelmed by fear that Gabe would go, that it wouldn't matter how old she'd said she was because she'd never see him again. Oblivious to everything else, she brooded for the remainder of their time on the ocean beach about that awful possibility.

As soon as the family returned to the cottage late that afternoon, she bolted from the car, saying, "I'll be back soon." Then she took off for the bay beach before her mother had time to object.

The tide was high. The only beach left was a small wedge, jammed full of families with small children. Bright colored sails tagged the gray water of the bay, but Kelsey didn't see anything identifiable as Gabe's Windsurfer.

The instant she walked into the cottage, her mother asked her, "What was that about?"

"Nothing. I just wanted to see the beach," Kelsey

said. She got her notepaper to take to the deck so that she could add to her letter to Jennifer.

"I feel so lonely smack in the middle of my own family," she wrote, "because I'm different from them. Even Ria thinks I'm weird now. Just because I pretended I was fifteen so that a boy would like me. You'd have done the same thing, wouldn't you? It's amazing that you're more like me than my own sister. But, oh, Jennifer, what if I never see him again?"

Mother rapped on the window behind Kelsey. "Kelsey, we're going to drive Ria over to the tennis courts and see what's happening there. Could you manage to watch Sara without fighting with her for an hour?"

"No problem," Kelsey said loftily. She waited for her mother to leave, then wrote, "Every time my mother asks me to do anything, she insults me. She really despises me. Not that she'd admit it. . . ."

The letter had grown to ten pages by the time Kelsey ran out of things to say. She ended with a plea for Jennifer to write back immediately and tucked the pages, crammed with her large curly script, into an envelope. It would probably need at least two stamps.

What was Sara doing anyway? Not a peep out of her. For all Kelsey, the baby-sitter, knew, Sara could have gone to the beach and swum straight out to sea. Well, at least the family would have to approve of her if she saved Sara from drowning.

"Sara," Kelsey called. She slid open the screen door to the living room and called again. No answer. It didn't take long to search the entire cottage. No little sister. "Sara!" Kelsey yelled from the top of the basement stairs.

"Just a minute," came a small, faraway voice.

Kelsey ran down the steep wooden stairs and immediately spotted Sara's bare toes poking out between the washing machine and the wall. A veil of smoke hung over the washing machine.

"What are you doing there?" Kelsey went over to see.

Sara was crouched next to the washing machine. Her brown eyes brimmed with guilt as she looked up at Kelsey, a lit cigarette in her hand. "I just wanted to see why Dad likes it. Want a puff?"

"No way, kid. You're not getting me in trouble, too."

"I'm not in trouble."

"You will be when I tell Dad you snitched his cigarettes and smoked them."

"Don't tell on me, Kelsey. Please." The big eyes were piteous. "I'll get killed."

Kelsey folded her arms. "And what are you going to do if I don't tell?"

"I don't know. What?"

Playing responsible big sister, Kelsey said, "You're going to promise never to smoke again."

"Oh, I won't. It tastes awful. I feel sick."

"Go lie down then." Kelsey held her hand out for the pack. "Where were these?"

"By the telephone."

Sara stumbled upstairs. She wouldn't be trying cigarettes again for a while, Kelsey thought as she sauntered toward the telephone on the kitchen counter.

The front door opened. Kelsey turned to see her father behind her. "Oh, hi, Dad."

His eyes fixed on the pack in her hand. "What are you doing with those?"

"Uh." She looked at him, stumped as she realized that she couldn't tell on Sara. "I was straightening up the kitchen and . . . I found them."

He looked doubtful. In came Mother, followed by Ria.

"Kelsey!" Mother said accusingly.

"I was not smoking. So don't even think it."

"What are you doing with those cigarettes then?"

The lie she'd told her father wasn't any more convincing the second time she used it. Mother advanced and told her to blow. Kelsey blew. Mom sniffed, but continued looking suspicious.

Dad took the pack from Kelsey's hand. "Listen," he said, "I know it's bad to say do as I say and not as I do, but please, Kelsey, don't start smoking. It's a rotten habit. As soon as things begin looking up for me again, I'm going to try to kick it."

"Your smoking has nothing to do with Kelsey," Mom said to him. "She shouldn't – "

"*I wasn't smoking!*" Kelsey screamed. "Why won't you believe me?"

She whirled and saw Sara peeking around the corner. "Say something," Kelsey mouthed silently at her sister. Sara backed away. Kelsey chased her through the living room and cornered her in the hall. "Tell them it was you," she whispered.

Sara shook her head, turning her lips in stubbornly.

"You stinker," Kelsey hissed. Then she raced out of the house. Always her, always. Anything bad that happened had to be her fault because she was the one they didn't trust. Anger dried the tears welling up in her. Anger sent her flying to the beach to be alone.

The tide had turned, exposing a narrow strip of wet brown sand all the way to the wider beach near the jetty. It was near dinnertime, and the only people around were a gray-haired couple hauling their Sunfish out of the water. Kelsey headed toward the point. She would walk over the bathtub-sized boulders all the way to the channel light at the end. There she'd sit until dark – until she died maybe.

She didn't notice the man in the chair next to the high dune grass, or realize that the boy crouched beside him rolling up the kite string was Gabe, until Herb Altman yelled: "Halloo, Kelsey." He waved for her to come over.

Her stomach flip-flopped as she approached them.

"Know anything about kite flying?" Herb asked.

"My father's the kite flyer," she said faintly.

"Well, what's your opinion? Gabe says I bought him a defective kite. I say he just doesn't know how to fly it."

She looked at the barely rippled water. "There probably isn't enough wind."

"One more try," Gabe said. "Here I go." He began to run with the kite which skipped along the ground instead of soaring. Muscles in the calves of his legs and upper arms rounded out his long, lean body. He was so beautiful.

"So tell me, Kelsey," Herb said, "what do *you* do for fun around here?"

"Nothing. Just come to the beach," Kelsey said.

"Women must be easier to entertain." Herb gave a sad smile at her confusion and explained, "I promised Gabe a great summer, but I'm already out of fun ideas. Maybe if he had someone his own age to talk to . . ." Herb jerked his eyebrows up and down in a humorous plea.

"Well, but I don't think he likes me."

"What do you mean? Not like you! You knock him dead every time he gets up the courage to sneak a peek."

"Now you're teasing me," Kelsey said and added indignantly, "I couldn't knock anybody dead. I've got red hair and freckles and besides, I'm too young."

Herb's smile was tender. "My first wife, Gabe's mother, had red hair and freckles."

"Did she die?" Kelsey asked respectfully.

"Not her. She's a college professor at the state university in Albany. Gabe lives with her."

"Oh." Suddenly Kelsey understood why it was so important to Herb Altman that Gabe enjoy himself.

"Ah!" He smiled, reading her mind. "I took you for the kind of woman who'd understand. Good. Well, I'm going for a snooze. You tell Gabe no need to hurry back to the cottage. Okay?"

"Okay," she agreed.

He rose from the chair, folded it and left, moving as if he were much older than he looked. Kelsey wondered if something was wrong with him. She hoped not. She liked him. And he'd said she was the kind of woman who understood. That was the best thing anyone had said to her in weeks.

Gabe came up to her, spooling the kite string again. "I guess you're right," he said. "There isn't enough wind."

"Your father said to tell you he's going for a nap."

Gabe nodded and kept rolling string.

"It's a beautiful kite," Kelsey said of the red, blue, and green nylon parafoil. "All my father ever gets are paper ones."

"Paper would have done fine for me," Gabe said. "Kites aren't my thing, really. You want to try it?"

"No thanks. I only like them up in the sky when somebody else gets them there." She paused, and then said, "Your father thinks you need somebody your age to talk to."

Gabe shook his head. "I wish he wouldn't try so hard to entertain me. I didn't come to be entertained. I was glad that he wanted to spend time with me. He's my father after all."

"He said you live with your mother."

"Yeah."

His tone warned her off. She tried something less personal. "Is Albany nice?"

"It's okay. We have an old town house right in the

city. There's always something going on in the streets, lots of interesting people. I could have had a job in an ice-cream shop if I'd stayed there this summer."

"Would you rather be home than here?"

"No," he said. "What gave you that idea?"

"Nothing . . . You look a lot like your father," she said.

"I know. And would you believe this is the first time we've ever been together? I don't know what made Mom decide it was okay. She never wanted me to have anything to do with him before."

"That's awful. I mean, he's your *father*."

"Yeah, parents can be hard to figure."

The statement was so true that she was encouraged to ask, "Do you ever feel as if you don't belong?"

Gabe thought about it carefully, then answered, "Not usually. Oh, maybe if I hit the wrong lunch table in school, but I always belong at home." His honey brown eyes tilted away from each other in an interesting way as he studied her. "How about you?"

"Me? I'm always on the outside in my family. It's like I'm trying to reach them through a thick glass window," Kelsey confessed. "I can't even talk to them."

"Why not?"

"Because they do things like accusing me of smoking when I haven't been."

"And you're Miss Innocent?" He grinned at her.

What could she say? Miss Innocent. She didn't want him to think she was boring. "Well," she fibbed, imagining her much older self, "maybe I smoke now and then or have a beer, like at a party, but I'm not — you know, a real hard case."

"Glad to hear it," Gabe said. "I didn't take you for a real hard case."

He was teasing her. She tacked in a safer direction by asking him a question. "Can you talk to your parents?"

"My mother and I are both private sort of people, but I can talk to her, yeah, about most things. And my father — well, we're still getting used to each other."

"He seems so easy to be with," she said.

"But he talks all the time, and that makes me clam up."

She asked if he was spending the whole summer here.

"He wanted it to be the whole summer," Gabe said, "but then, something came up and now he says a month — Well, that's fine with me."

"You miss your mother?"

"Not really. I may be an only child, but I'm not a mama's boy. Usually I go to camp summers, and Mom works on grants or travels or something."

"I wish *I* were an only child."

"Me, I wish I had brothers and sisters."

She chewed her lip, considering. It would be easy, at this point, to mention that she had an older sister his age. If his father had relayed her lie, she could say he'd misunderstood her, but then what about her boast that she smoked and drank sometimes? "I've got two sisters," Kelsey said cautiously. "The young-est one's a brat, and the other one, she's pluperfect proper like my mother."

He laughed. "Pluperfect proper huh?"

"Why didn't you want to talk to me this morning?" she asked to steer him away from Ria. "I mean, you wouldn't even look at me."

"I looked." His lips twitched in that almost smile. "But I was uptight about making a fool of myself on the Windsurfer the first time."

"You were good. You made it look easy."

"Umm. If I could rent it again — but I hate taking advantage of my father. He's not very rich. I mean, from how he described his apartment to me, and he doesn't take vacations or anything — until this sum-mer."

"He's worried you'll get bored here," she said.

"I won't. The beach is all I need."

"Me too. This is my favorite place in the whole world."

"You mean you've checked out every other?" he teased.

"I know what I like."

"I bet you do."

When he said he ought to go back, Kelsey's spirits sank, but they revived when he suggested they meet on the beach at ten the next morning. "You could bring your sisters. I'd like to meet them," Gabe said.

"Oh, no, you wouldn't," she told him. Unbidden, another lie flew out of her mouth. "Anyway, Ria's got a boyfriend."

His brows came together questioningly as if he wondered why she'd thrown that in. She couldn't very well explain that it was to keep him from liking Ria better than her when he met the older, cooler, prettier sister.

"Well," she said in a hurry to be gone before she said anything worse, "see you then."

She'd reached the road and was almost to Aunt Syl's pitch-pine-covered backyard before the lies she'd told caught up with her. The only beer she'd ever tasted had been from her father's can at a ballgame, and tobacco smelled so vile to her that she'd never tried smoking. Idiot, she told herself. Liar. What a phony you are!

But his father had said that she'd knocked him dead. Did that mean she was pretty? Sometimes she thought she might be, and her friends claimed she was. Gabe wasn't as hard to talk to as some boys she knew, maybe because he was older. And he was good-looking and probably smart. Oh, yes, she was lucky, but not because of her family. Somehow she was going to have to hide them from him so that he didn't uncover her lies.

Gabe! Tonight she'd write Cathy a letter and tell her about the boy she'd met on the beach. Gabe and Kelsey. Even their names went well together.

4

She felt so happy. She felt so lucky. She felt winged with delight, returning to the cottage from her encounter with Gabe. Her parents were sitting on the deck. "Did you get the mail? Was there anything for me?" she sang out when she saw the letter in her father's hand.

Mom lowered her newspaper and peered at Kelsey over the top of her half glasses. "Where were you? I sent Ria to find you, but she didn't see you on the beach."

"I was there."

"Kelsey, your sister said she checked every head in the water, and you know Ria's thorough."

"I went for a walk down to the jetty."

"Did you? And what happened to the rule about telling us where you're going?"

"I was upset." Kelsey's spirits sank as she remembered why.

"We're upset too," Mom said. "Your father and I have been sitting here trying to figure out what to do with you."

"What do you mean what to do with me? What am

I now, a criminal or something because I didn't tell you where I was going?"

Mother snorted in disgust and said, "You talk to her, Ralph." But she wasn't one to let someone else fight her battles. Before he could begin, she leaned toward Kelsey and said, "I've never had a student who'd dare talk to me the way you do. If you don't start showing me some respect, you're going to find your privileges restricted, Kelsey Morris."

"What privileges?" Kelsey asked. "I didn't know I had any."

"Is that so? Don't you think being part of a healthy family who feed, clothe, and care for you is a privilege? Believe me, many children in this world would be grateful."

"You think I'm so awful, Mom. Why don't you kick me out? You could stick me with foster parents, and I bet *they'd* think I was great."

"Listen to her!" Mom turned to her husband. "She means it. Now do you wonder why I say I've failed as a mother?"

"Enough." Dad stood up and took Kelsey's arm and sat her down in his deck chair facing him. "Freedom of choice is one privilege you have in this family, Kelsey, and you're abusing it," he began earnestly. "You run off whenever you feel like it without telling us where you're going. From now on, you're going to ask permission before you step out of this house. Also, you will speak politely to us. I know you can do it because I've heard you with your friends."

"My friends speak politely to me."

"Quiet!" he boomed. "As for the smoking, I do consider that a criminal act because you did it when you were supposed to be in charge of your little sister, and you set a bad example for her."

Kelsey folded her arms and said wearily, "I was not smoking. You don't believe me, but I wasn't."

"Lying, smoking – " Dad sounded grieved. "You better cool your heels in the house tomorrow, kid. You're grounded. Going to the beach is a privilege and you've lost it."

"Not tomorrow!" she cried, thinking of Gabe. "Please, not tomorrow. I'll be good. I'll be an angel, but please – I met someone I'm seeing tomorrow."

"You met someone? Who?" Mother asked.

"A boy, a very nice boy. You'd like him, Mom. He's polite and intelligent. He's here with his father."

"Fine. I'll be glad to meet him. You *do* remember that we expect to meet your friends?"

Kelsey opened her mouth and closed it. She couldn't win on that one without agreeing to introduce Gabe soon, which was just what she had to avoid. "No matter what I say, I get in trouble," she complained. "Whatever I do, you think it's wrong. You really hate me."

"I don't hate you, but I wish you weren't so wild."

"Wild? How am I wild?" Kelsey cried.

"Kelsey, keep your voice down," Mother said.

"But you said wild. Wild is a kid who drinks and smokes and does drugs and sex, and I haven't done any of those things."

"Except smoke," Dad said.

She was so tempted to tell him to ask Sara about that, so tempted. But squealing on her sister was against her principles, and whatever her parents might think, she did have principles. Taking a deep breath, she asked, "Can I go inside now?"

"Go ahead," Dad said. "You got a couple of letters from your friends. They're on the counter."

"Ria said it's your turn to set the table, Kelsey," Mother added.

Kelsey picked up the letters and held them to her cheek as if her friends' affection could seep through the paper to warm her. The pink self-folding note was from Cathy, and the blue envelope with a unicorn on the back was from Jennifer. Instead of reading them immediately, Kelsey decided to hoard the treat for later. Besides, the table must be set.

As she tucked the letters under her pillow, she heard Ria reading to Sara behind the closed door of Sara's bedroom. Brat, Kelsey thought angrily. Sara didn't have a smidgen of conscience to sit back and let her take the rap like this.

Her skin felt itchy from dried salt. She was still in the bathing suit she'd worn to the ocean beach. It wouldn't hurt to take a quick shower before she set the table.

"Kelsey, Dad wants to take a picture," Ria said at the bedroom doorway a few minutes later as Kelsey was getting into her jeans.

"My hair's wet. I can't."

"Grandma asked. Dad says she complained her last pictures of us are a year old. Come on. It'll only take a minute."

"The annual couch shot. When did it ever take a minute?"

Ria shrugged. Kelsey beckoned her sister closer. "I'm being punished for something I didn't do, Ria. It was Sara who tried out Dad's cigarettes." Ria looked surprised. "Would you talk to her?"

"You expect *me* to get her to confess?"

"Please! They're grounding me because of the smoking, and remember that boy I told you I met — Gabe? Well, I just made a date to meet him on the beach tomorrow, and if I don't show up, he'll think I don't like him or something."

"All right. All right. I'll try, but don't expect much. You know how chicken-hearted Sara is."

Kelsey hugged her older sister. "You're my only hope."

"Relax," Ria said, wriggling out of the embrace, uncomfortable as usual with physical affection. "This isn't a life-and-death matter. The parents won't stay mad long."

"Long enough to ruin my love life," Kelsey said.

In the living room, she sagged onto the couch in the annual photo position, with Sara poised like a show-dog on the edge of the seat between her older sisters. Dad began fussing with his camera settings. He did not snap pictures; he took them seriously. Kelsey had suggested they buy him a self-focusing camera for

Christmas, but Mom claimed he enjoyed the challenge of all those light and speed and lens focus options. His portraits would be a lot better if he didn't wear out his subjects before he clicked the shutter, Kelsey had said more than once. But, of course, no one listened to her. She ran her fingers through her wet hair. Maybe it would dry if Dad took long enough.

Mother was frowning at her. "Your hair's a mess," she said.

"I washed it. I can't brush it till it's dry." Kelsey stood up remembering she was supposed to be polite. "But I'll try if you want me to."

"Sit down," Mom said. "You didn't set the table either."

"I was going to as soon as I got dressed. Should I do it now?" Kelsey stood up again.

Mom groaned. Dad said, "Everybody sit down and smile."

Obediently, Kelsey sat and poked up the ends of her lips. Grandma lived in Seattle with her second husband. She flew East once a year at Christmas and gave them nice presents and blunt critical reviews on their growth and development. She didn't understand how Kelsey had gotten so many freckles and why she had red hair, or why Ria was so quiet, but she thought Sara was adorable.

Grandma was Mother's mother. They didn't get along. Grandma thought Mother's hair was too short and her clothes too dowdy. She had a habit she called honesty which allowed her to mention that the turkey wasn't as fresh as it might be and that the coffee was too strong. Mother always acted relieved when Grandma left.

"Okay, one more picture now," Dad said. "Sara, sit on the arm of the chair and lean toward your sisters this time. Kelsey, straighten up. You're sitting all hunched over, and your hair's in your face."

Kelsey quivered. Why couldn't Herb Altman be her father? He didn't think she was a lump. He thought she was pretty. She straightened up. "Do you think you could smile?" Dad asked her.

Tears filled her eyes.

"Kelsey, what's the matter with you?" Mom said.

"I can't help it," Kelsey got out before the sobs took over.

"Forget it," Dad said, losing patience. "Just forget it. Your grandmother will have to make do with last year's picture. I've had enough of this nonsense."

By the time Kelsey had cried herself out on her bed, her hair was dry. She brushed it vigorously before returning to the living room. Someone had set the table, and they were quietly eating dinner without her. Kelsey hung back. Maybe meals were a privilege the official family bad girl was to be denied.

"It's spaghetti," Mom turned to say. She smiled. "Your favorite. Why don't you have some before it gets cold."

"Thank you," Kelsey said with careful courtesy. As she sat down, her eyes happened to meet Sara's. Guiltily, Sara dropped her head until her nose was about an inch above her spaghetti and she couldn't see Kelsey anymore. Ria was neatly rolling spaghetti onto a fork.

"Sara set the table for you," Mother said.

"Wasn't that nice of you, Sara," Kelsey said, eyeing her sister hard.

Sara sucked in a spaghetti strand in silence, refusing to meet Kelsey's eyes.

After dinner Kelsey did the dishes, like a true penitent, while Ria took Sara for a walk. Ria gave Kelsey a wink over her shoulder as she ushered their youngest sister out the door. It wouldn't be long before Sara learned what Ria's real purpose for the walk was.

Kelsey retired to her bed to savor her still unopened letters while the parents watched news on TV. Cathy's letter was all about how she had bumped heads in a swimming pool with the boy who'd had a crush on Kelsey all spring, and how he'd asked Cathy to go to a movie with him and then didn't want to talk about anything but Kelsey. "And it was my first real date too," Cathy wrote. "Is it okay if I tell him you don't like his chin?" Kelsey giggled. Tell him I'm only interested in older men, she'd write back.

Jennifer's letter was satisfyingly long. Like Kelsey, she could talk for pages on paper. "You won't believe how religious I'm getting, Kelsey," she wrote and hinted that she was even thinking of becoming a nun. "God has to be a better husband than most of the ones I see, except maybe your father." Jennifer had a crush on Kelsey's father. She didn't remember her own, and Kelsey had never been able to convince her friend that Dad could be pretty unreasonable sometimes.

On the last page Jennifer talked about baby-sitting, and how she'd only gotten the baby to sleep a minute before the parents returned. "When they asked if he was a good boy, I said, 'Oh, sure, just fine,' and so now they want me to come back next week, but I don't know if I can stand a night like that again even though I do need the money. Maybe I'll tell them I'm sick or something."

There, Kelsey thought. That was a lie, and Jennifer was going to be a nun, too. Maybe. Everybody lied a little. Kelsey was no worse than anyone else, except maybe pluperfect honest Ria.

Ria came in just then and closed the door behind her. "Well, I did my best," she said, "but it's hopeless, Kelsey. Sara's scared because the parents were so hard on you. She thinks if they find out she smoked, they'll kill her. She feels bad that you're taking the blame, but not bad enough to turn herself in."

Kelsey nodded. It was what she expected.

Too bad, she thought when she saw the sunshine the next morning. If it had been raining, Gabe wouldn't have expected her to keep their date, but it was another perfect beach day.

At breakfast, Dad talked about renting a rowboat and taking them all flounder fishing. Kelsey was almost glad she was grounded so that she couldn't go.

She hated being confined to a small boat and pulling in fish that flopped painfully on the hook. Nobody could convince her that having a hook in your mouth wasn't painful.

"Do I have to stay in the whole day?" Kelsey asked in her most pathetic voice. "Couldn't I just go down to the beach for an hour and breathe some fresh sea air?"

"Sorry," Dad said as if he really was. "A punishment's a punishment."

"Half an hour? Mom?"

"Kelsey, it's only one day. You can breathe on the deck. You'll survive."

Sighing loudly, Kelsey sank into a chair. When they left, she was reading, but Sara made the mistake of returning for her hat. She was slinking past Kelsey in the living room as unobtrusively as possible when Kelsey said, "Don't you care that I'm being punished for what you did?"

"I'm sorry," Sara squeaked, caught in mid slink.

"If you were really sorry, you'd tell them."

"I can't."

"Okay, if you can live with yourself, okay. Then this is your sister, signing off forever." Kelsey zipped her finger across her lips to show she was finished talking. Sara hunched into herself and sidled off like a hermit crab, but Kelsey knew better than to feel sorry for her. She'd forget the minute she hit the car. They'd all forget. They were probably glad the family troublemaker wasn't with them.

She put her book down. If only Gabe had a phone

and she knew the number, she could call and invite him over. She'd still be grounded. Only she'd be having fun instead of suffering unjustly. What was Gabe doing now? It would only take a minute to run over to the beach and see, one little minute or two. Would that be so terrible? She wasn't even guilty. It didn't make sense to honor the terms of a punishment she didn't deserve.

She wished she could call Jennifer and ask her opinion. For instance, suppose the house were burning. The parents wouldn't expect her to stay inside and die. Of course not. And if she could see the bay from the cottage and somebody were drowning, they'd be proud of her if she left the house to go and save that person.

If Ria were here, Kelsey could write a note and have her take it to Gabe, and then he'd come, and they'd sit on the deck, and she'd still be obeying the rules, but — but then Ria would meet him and he'd probably fall for her. She was blond and better-looking than Kelsey and smarter and more athletic. Swimming and getting in trouble were Kelsey's only abilities. Besides Ria was fifteen, and she didn't have a steady boyfriend. Kelsey had only said she did to keep Gabe from becoming interested in her. Another stupid lie! She was getting to be almost as bad as Mom thought she was.

Kelsey sat up straight. What was she sitting there thinking about? She had a perfect setup. She'd go find Gabe herself and invite him to her deck. No need to introduce him to the family. No need to unground herself, either – except for the few minutes it would take to run to the beach, locate him, and return. Five minutes tops. Besides, she was innocent.

Excited, she went to put on her best white shorts. They were stained, but her purple T-shirt covered the spots. She brushed her long red hair until it crackled, then raced her conscience across the road to the beach.

5

He wasn't at the beach. A flotilla of plastic inflatable dinosaurs and ducks with small children attached were there, but no Gabe. The water sparkled with an invitation that Kelsey resisted. She felt guilty enough standing next to the concrete retaining wall looking for Gabe when she'd promised not to leave the cottage. Where *was* he? Unless – what if he was waiting for her way down the beach at the jetty?

Impulsively, she raced off in that direction, as if she were trying to outrun misgivings. A Windsurfer winged out past the long line of rocks marking the entrance to Wellfleet Harbor. The silhouetted figure on it probably wasn't Gabe, she decided, since she didn't see his father keeping watch from shore. She pounded past a young couple slathering sunscreen on each other, and a fisherman whose stomach pouched like a mailbag over his belt.

Finally, she stopped to catch her breath and consider. So Gabe wasn't on the beach. He could still come. It was early yet. Only now her conscience caught up with her, and instead of waiting, she hurried back to the cottage. She lunged inside gasping and was relieved to see by the kitchen clock that she'd only been gone fifteen minutes. Against the total hours of her jail sentence, fifteen minutes didn't even count. But why hadn't he come? He'd found something better to do for sure – or someone better to be with.

She trailed off to the bathroom to wash her flushed face. The scowling image in the mirror was not pretty, and the red hair frizzed around her forehead again. It wouldn't stay smooth in the damp sea air. Why couldn't she be blond like Ria or even dark and silky-haired like Sara? And to have freckles like a spotted giraffe besides! No wonder Gabe hadn't come.

Back in the kitchen, Kelsey stared bleakly at the clock. Just ten, which was when he'd said they should meet. He might be there now, or maybe he'd be coming a few minutes late. It had been foolish to go looking for him so early. She drank a glass of water, thinking. What if she made another dash, just to the edge of the beach and back. Would five more minutes of ungrounding herself be so bad?

She hesitated over the answer. The morning was so still that she could hear a clink as the man painting shutters on the cottage across the lane dipped his brush in his paint pail. A car swished past on the beach road behind Aunt Syl's lot. Kelsey took a deep breath. One more trip, just one. So long as she spent *most* of the day in the house, she'd still be obediently submitting to her punishment, her unjust punishment.

Off she ran again. Today she was getting enough exercise to meet Ria's approval.

The beach was more crowded, but no long-limbed boy with muscular arms and bony shoulders awaited her there. Kelsey groaned in frustration. If only she could leave him a message. In the sand she told herself. The tide was going out. Toddlers puddled about on the right side of the beach, but near the water to the left was an unused stretch of wet brown sand. She used her big toe to write in foot high letters, "Where are you, Gabe?" and signed it "K." Glancing over her shoulder as she left the beach, she was dismayed to see a small boy, with sailboat in hand, making footprints right across her message.

This whole frustrating, miserable morning was Sara's fault. If Sara had owned up to being the smoker, Kelsey might be swimming with Gabe now instead of chasing back and forth like a maniac. Probably she'd never even see Gabe again. She hoped bratty Sara got bitten by a flounder. Never mind that flounders had no teeth.

From the open doorway of her little sister's room, Kelsey could see First Turtle on Sara's pillow. His quilted green and yellow body was frayed and shabby. A fiendish idea came to her. What if she held First Turtle hostage until Sara confessed to the parents? Except, Sara would tell the parents who the kidnapper was first. Unless. Unless Kelly threatened she'd tell who'd really been smoking if Sara went to the parents about First Turtle. That was it.

Kelsey was just sorry she hadn't thought of it sooner. She snatched up First Turtle and looked around her own bedroom for a hiding place. It had to be a good one or Sara'd get him back without having to pay up. Under the bed was too easy. The back of the closet was too obvious. Kelsey tried the basement.

Beneath the stairs was a huge, speckled blue enamel lobster pot. Perfect-o!

Feeling better, she took her mystery book out to the deck, but she couldn't concentrate. She kept thinking about Gabe, wondering why he hadn't come. At noon she checked the clock again and ate some crackers with peanut butter. The family should be home soon, but she might squeeze in another run to the beach, just in case something had delayed him and he was looking for her.

This time she strolled the few hundred feet to the beach entrance. Her message was still visible, Xed over with a crosshatch of footprints, but legible. She blinked. Something had been written below it. She ran to see. "Where are you, Gabe? K" was hers, but after it in neat, deeply etched letters was, "Gabe here, where are you, K?"

Then he'd come! He'd really come. Off she flew to the jetty again. And there, at last, she saw him. He was stretched out on his stomach on the sand near the rocks next to a Windsurfer. She wondered if it was the one she'd seen on the water that morning. It could be.

"Was sailing fun?" she asked the prone figure.

He turned over and sat up. A smile creased his lean face ear to ear. "We missed each other," he said.

"I just got your message."

"Before I found yours, I thought you'd stood me up."

"Oh, I'd never do that. Never," she assured him.

They kept smiling, and watching each other smiling, until Kelsey felt giddy.

"Hey, why don't you sit down?" he said.

She sat next to him — just for a moment, she told herself — and asked where his father was.

The smile disappeared and Gabe's face darkened. "He said he was tired. I don't know what from. He's probably still in bed."

Sensing that something was bothering him, Kelsey asked, "This isn't really the very first time you ever were with Herb, is it?"

"Yup." All of a sudden his control broke and it spilled out of him in a flood of words. "See, he and my mother had a bad divorce. Nasty. She got custody, but he had visiting rights. Not that he bothered using them. Mom said it took him ten years to finally get interested in being a father. Then she told him it was too late and she wouldn't let him see me . . . well, but I think then she was worried that he'd charm me, because when I was ten, I really wanted a father bad. *Now,* she probably expects I can see through him better. At least, I think that's why she's letting me spend time with him this summer."

"*Do* you see through him?"

Gabe laughed. "No . . . Except that he talks too much, he seems like a really neat guy. Of course, when somebody's knocking himself out to give you a good time, it's hard not to think he's nice."

"It must feel so strange," Kelsey mused, "not to know your own father."

"It is strange. I used to wonder what he was like. I used to dream about meeting him, and now here we are, and it's like I'm still dreaming, you know?"

Kelsey nodded. "So why did he decide to look you up?"

Gabe shrugged. "Beats me. I haven't asked him."

"Really? I'd be curious."

"Yeah, well, it's a good question. . . . I'll ask him and tell you what he says." Gabe gestured at the Windsurfer. "Want to try it?"

"Not me, thanks."

"Not much of a swimmer?"

"Oh, I can swim. It's my only sport. My sister Ria's a tennis champ, and she's a good all-round athlete, and my little sister Sara does gymnastics. But I'm not much at anything. I mean I don't excel."

"How about in school?"

She shook her head, but she said, "I'm a good friend. That's my best thing. I like people."

"Do you?" Gabe considered. Then he said, "I don't like everybody. I guess I'm discriminating. There are some guys I ski with and my partner in science lab. . . . And I like you."

She blinked at the compliment and banked it for later.

"How about going for a swim with me now?" Gabe said.

Suddenly, she remembered her parents and leaped to her feet. "Oh, no, I can't."

He stood up too and said, "Well, I could walk you back to your cottage so you could get a suit."

"No, that's not it. See, I'm supposed to be grounded, and if my parents don't find me home, I'm in trouble."

One eyebrow went up over his tilted, asymmetrical eyes. "What'd you do?"

"Nothing. My little sister was smoking, and they thought it was me and that I was lying about it besides."

"Oh." His face cleared. "And you didn't tell them it was your sister? Sara's her name, right?"

"I couldn't do *that*. That'd be rotten."

"Would it? Well, what would I know being an only child." He grinned. "So when do I get to meet these sisters of yours?"

"Uh. Soon. Maybe . . . Gabe, I have to run."

"Right. Go ahead. I'll see you later."

She was racing away down the beach when she heard him yelling. She stopped and turned. "What?"

He made a megaphone of his hands to shout, "When?"

"Tomorrow morning after breakfast. Here."

He waved and she took off again. It was midafternoon, judging by how near the sun was to the green and tan hills of Chequesset Neck across the harbor. The parents would be home, and they'd be furious that she wasn't. Bad luck, just the worst luck.

She grasped the deck railing as if it were the finish line of a race. No car. Good! They weren't home yet. She dropped onto the step breathing hard and barely had time to catch her breath before the car pulled into the crushed shell driveway.

"Sorry we're so late," Dad said through the open window.

"We only started catching fish after lunch," Mom said. She got out with the plastic bucket and tipped it so that Kelsey could see. "Fish for dinner tonight."

"And breakfast, too, it looks like," Kelsey said with dismay.

"I caught three," Sara boasted.

"Ria caught the most," Mom said.

It had never ceased to amaze Kelsey that her sisters actually liked fishing. "Am I still grounded?" she asked.

Her mother looked at her father, then said, "I guess you've done your time. Go ahead. You can get in a swim before dinner while we clean all these fish."

"Unless you'd care to help clean them," Dad said.

"No way!" Kelsey bounded into the house and changed into her suit. If Gabe were still on the beach, they could do that swim together after all.

She was about to leave when she heard Sara squealing in her bedroom, "First Turtle's gone."

"Umm," Kelsey stepped into the room to say, "I guess he didn't want to hang around with a little girl who'd let somebody else take the blame for what she did."

"First Turtle can't leave me. He's *stuffed*," said Sara the realist. "You took him, Kelsey, didn't you?"

"Yes, but you can get him back by telling Dad who was smoking his cigarettes yesterday. That is if you *want* First Turtle back."

Kelsey made sure that Sara understood the consequences of identifying First Turtle's kidnapper before she sauntered out of the cottage with her towel in hand. She imagined Sara ransacking the house in her search for the hostage. Sara'd never think of the lobster pot under the stairs.

Gabe was nowhere in sight when Kelsey got to the beach, but she consoled herself with the thought that she'd spend tomorrow morning with him, and day after day for a month thereafter.

Late afternoon was her favorite time at the beach. Then the sunlight mellowed. Sea and sky were serene, and it was still warm enough to swim. Everyone had gone to shower away salt and sand and eat supper, and the beach belonged to the gulls and her. Why she should love that solitude, when she'd rather be with people most anywhere else, was a mystery that Kelsey didn't feel a need to solve.

She ran knee deep into the greenish water and did a shallow dive. Then she swam from the breakwater on the right side of the beach to the shorter one on the left. Back and forth, lap after lap, buoyed by the salty water. A school of three-inch-long bait fish zipped by beneath her nose like blips on a television screen. The occasional pinkish blob of jellyfish didn't faze her, and the water was clear of seaweed today. She glided through it, mesmerized by her own smooth flowing motion, content with life for a change.

Her wet hair was plastered to her shoulders and her stomach was growling with hunger when she came out. Not hungry enough for the flounder, of course. She'd make herself a melted cheese sandwich for dinner instead, and Mom would make her usual comment, something like, "You might just as well have been born a mouse, for all the variety in your diet."

Sara was sitting on the front steps. Her cheeks were tearstained. As soon as she saw Kelsey, she said, "Now can I have First Turtle back? I told them."

"You did?"

"And I'm sorry. I mean, I really am sorry even though they said I had to say it. I really, really am."

"See, it wasn't so bad to fess up, was it?"

"Yes, it was. Mom and Dad are so mad at me!" Sara broke into noisy sobs.

Kelsey patted her back, dismayed by the depth of Sara's misery. "Don't worry. They'll forget, and by tomorrow they'll think you're the cutest kid in the world again. Believe me."

Sara's sobs only slowed to sniffles when Kelsey promised, "I'll get First Turtle."

A minute later Sara was hugging her treasure, happy again.

Dad came through the hall and looked at Kelsey

shamefaced. "Honey, I'm sorry. I was sure Sara was too little to — I'm really very sorry I didn't believe you."

Kelsey nodded and said, "You should believe me, Dad. I'm basically a truthful person." But recalling her deceptions of the last two days, she amended that. "Well, mostly when it's important to be truthful I am."

"How about a kiss to show I'm forgiven?" Dad asked.

While she was kissing her father, Kelsey saw her mother watching them from the kitchen where she was rolling flounder fillets in milk and flour.

"Anyone who thinks being a mother is easy should try it in this family for a week," Mother said.

Kelsey was indignant. "Is that all you can say after what you did to me? You stuck me in the house for a whole beautiful beach day!"

"Well, I still don't like the way you talk to me, Kelsey, and I still don't like it that you're never where you're supposed to be."

"But? Not even a 'but'?" Kelsey asked indignantly.

"I'm sorry you got punished for something you didn't do, yes."

"Thank you," Kelsey said. "Sorry is something at least."

"You see," Mom said in annoyance. "There you go again with that snippy tone."

"Whoah, whoah." Dad waved his arms. "Not another fight this soon. Wait till after dinner, at least."

Kelsey went off to shower. She was pulling on jeans and a sweatshirt when Ria came into the room.

"It's hard for Mom to apologize when she's wrong, at least to us," Ria said. "But she feels bad. I know she does."

"No, she doesn't. She doesn't care how rotten she treats me. I'm just Kelsey, her worst daughter, and she wishes I'd never been born."

"Kelsey, come on. Don't be that way. Dad said he was sorry."

Kelsey brushed the whole subject of her parents aside impatiently to say, "Ria, I saw Gabe for just a little this afternoon, and now he wants to meet my family. He still doesn't know how old I am. What am I going to do?"

Ria chewed her thumbnail. "You saw Gabe? I thought you were grounded."

"Well, I was. I only ran to the beach for a minute to tell him I couldn't keep our date."

"But you weren't supposed to leave the house."

"Ria, whose side are you on?"

"Well — " she began and stopped.

"Well what?"

"Well, nothing. I don't know. You'll think of something. As to how old you are, maybe when he finds out, he'll like you enough to keep liking you anyway."

"You won't help me?"

Ria looked sympathetic, but she said, "I don't see how I can."

Kelsey moaned. Somehow, she had to arrange it so

that Gabe didn't meet her family. Maybe she could tell him they'd all gone home. Except he'd bump into one or the other of them sometime for sure. She could say they were stricken with an infectious disease. But she wasn't going to lie anymore, was she? How about if she convinced him they wouldn't like him if they met him. But why wouldn't they like him, adorable as he was? The amazing thing was that he'd even talk to a red-haired, freckle-faced, awkward, thirteen-year-old semihonest person like herself. Luck, she thought — she needed luck to keep things going her way.

6

In her nightmare, an enormous green slippery-sided wave was about to topple over on Kelsey. She struggled to escape it while on the beach, Mom showed Gabe a pink frosted birthday cake decorated with the number thirteen.

Kelsey sat bolt upright in bed, breathing hard. Just a dream, she reassured herself. In the dim light, she could see the outline of Ria's straight back. Outside the sky was pink. Kelsey blinked in wonder, and tip-toed to the window to witness the sunrise. The bluffs across the marsh toward Route 6 were illuminated with rosy light, and birds were exuberantly cheering the coming of day. She felt like cheering too as she remembered that in a few hours she would be meeting Gabe on the beach.

Ria's pink hairbrush lay on the dresser, but Kelsey couldn't find her own. Easing her drawer open, she poked around unsuccessfully in the tumble of clothes. Silly that Ria was so touchy about sharing personal things like brushes and towels. It was cozy to share with someone you loved.

Kelsey fingered Ria's brush, listening to her even

breathing. So long as every last copper hair was removed, Ria wouldn't know, and no harm would be done. Slowly, Kelsey pulled the pink plastic brush through her tangled hair. The long, soothing strokes massaged her scalp. She finished as dawn faded into day, cleaned the brush out with her fingers and put it back exactly where she'd found it.

Her own brush was hiding behind the tissue box on the toilet tank. She cleaned her teeth and returned to her room to get dressed, brush in hand. There was baby sister perched on Ria's bed. "What are *you* doing up, Sara?" Kelsey asked.

"She says she saw you using my brush again," Ria said grumpily. Her eyes were still half shut.

Stalling, Kelsey said, "Me?" She held her own brush up as evidence of her innocence.

Immediately, Ria's annoyance veered to her youngest sister. "Why are you trying to get Kelsey in trouble again, Sara?"

"I wasn't. I went by to go to the bathroom, and saw her. I know it was your brush 'cause yours is pink and hers is square." As if it would prove something, Sara bounced off the bed and brought Ria's brush to her.

Afraid she'd left an incriminating hair, Kelsey dived for the brush and tried to wrestle it away from Sara.

"Stop it. Stop it, you two. You'll wake up the parents," Ria hissed and grabbed Sara, pinning her arms to her side.

"You're hurting me," Sara whimpered.

"I am not."

"You little fink," Kelsey said. "You're the worst

little sister in the world. Why do you always have to make trouble for me?"

"What's all the racket about?" Dad demanded. He stood in the doorway in his pajamas looking as grouchy as Ria had at being awakened too early.

"Kelsey's calling me names, Daddy."

"And Sara's making trouble between Ria and me *deliberately*," Kelsey complained.

"You girls are noisier than a flock of migrating geese," Dad said. "Go to bed fighting. Wake up fighting. Go back to sleep — all of you." He tromped back to bed.

"Out," Ria told Sara.

"But she was using your — "

"Out!" Ria pointed sternly toward the door. Sara left with downturned lips and an injured look.

"She's such a brat," Kelsey said.

"*Did* you use my brush, Kelsey?"

"Just a couple of swipes, and I cleaned it out. I couldn't find mine."

"I wish I had brothers." Ria thumped her pillow with her fist. "Brothers would be much easier to live with." Her head followed her fist as she dove back into sleep.

Kelsey was wide awake and restless. "Ria," she said. "I have an idea about Gabe. Would you listen for a minute?"

"No."

Kelsey sat down on the floor next to the bed, and whispered into her sister's ear. "If you met him, and said he was nice, Mom would believe you. She trusts your judgment. You wouldn't have to lie or anything because he *is* nice. And you wouldn't have to lie to him either — just not mention age." Except, Kelsey thought, what if Gabe brought up the boyfriend Ria was supposed to have? But most likely he wouldn't.

"Go away." Ria swatted Kelsey with her pillow.

Discouraged, Kelsey drifted into the living room. It was dreary being the only one awake in a cottage full of sleepers. She was tempted to see how the beach looked this early, but she was still wearing her pajamas, and she'd wake Ria again if she returned for her clothes.

A hard lump at the back of the couch cushion poked Kelsey's rump. She reached behind her and found her diary. Terrific! It had vanished the first day they'd arrived, and she'd given up looking for it. Her diary was for venting feelings too embarrassing to confide to friends, evil thoughts, and anything that might be ridiculous. So far she had filled three books. This red leatherette-covered one with impressive gold-edged pages was new. She found a pen and settled comfortably into the writing.

"My childhood is about over, and I'm glad because it wasn't happy. Well, maybe the first six years were okay when my father loved me, but then my little sister got born. Sure, I'm not perfect, but it's rotten the way everyone in my family has it in for me. Even Ria gets mad at me for nothing. Like using her hairbrush. How ridiculous! I wash my hair more than she does.

"Sometimes I hate myself. I wonder if it's really me and not them. I don't know who to blame, but I know they ought to like me better than they do because I'm a nice person. Well, not all the time, but anyway . . . I bet if I were in a different family, they'd like me."

She stopped writing. Suppose, just suppose, she happened to leave the diary out, like on the low table in front of the couch. Ria and Dad probably wouldn't read it; they had principles. But Mother and Sara would be sure to peek.

Kelsey thought, then wrote, "The worst one in the family is my little sister. She spends her whole life getting me in trouble. Then they think I'm not nice to her when she's the one who's mean to me.

"As for my mother, she'll never say, 'I love you,' not to me, and never ever ever will she admit I have good points. Like – " Kelsey stopped writing to think. Offhand she couldn't come up with any good points. She scratched out "like." A minute's chewing on the end of the pen yielded, "Mother says I smart mouth her, but what about the things she says to me?"

Enough, Kelsey decided. She didn't want to make it so long they'd be discouraged from reading it. She closed the diary with the pen inside as page marker and left it in the middle of the table where it couldn't be missed.

Quietly, she made herself an English muffin for breakfast. Having finished off the last glass of orange juice, she considerately left a can of frozen juice defrosting on the counter next to a note saying she'd gone to the beach. Then, slipping her father's denim jacket over her pajamas, she set off barefooted in the cool of early morning.

A mockingbird dipped its tail and flew off, flashing white markings at her. Two rabbits, nibbling grass behind a split-rail fence along the sand road, watched her pass. When she got to the beach, the air had a soft luster, and she could see all the way across the bay to the remains of the target ship off Eastham. A seagull, breakfasting on the wet sand, flew up with a clam and dropped it on a rock. She waited until the gull managed to crack the clam open. Then, feeling calm and happy, she started home.

A car stopped behind her as she was crossing the road. "Kelsey." It was Herb calling. Gabe was sitting beside him. "What are you doing up so early?"

"Do you know seagulls drop clams on rocks to break them open?"

"No kidding!" Herb said. "And we think we're so smart."

"We don't think you're so smart this morning, Dad," Gabe teased him.

"Just because I burned a few pancakes? Can you believe this kid, Kelsey? I'm treating him to a pancake breakfast in town, and he's still giving me a hard time."

"Sounds like a good deal to me," she said.

"Join us then," Herb offered.

"No, thanks," she said quickly, thinking of the pajamas hidden beneath her father's voluminous jacket. "I mean, that's really nice of you, but I've had breakfast."

"Which is your place?" Herb wanted to know.

Reluctantly Kelsey pointed. "It's just through those trees past the SLOW, CHILDREN sign. It's too small to see from the road."

"We're in one of the shacks on the hill back there. Talk about small," Herb chatted, "when one of us moves his legs, the other one gets kicked. Come over later, and we'll show you."

"Kelsey's going for a swim with me later, Dad."

"Well, how about that! And here I thought you two needed a go-between. Well, fine. Then, how about coming over after the swim and we'll have lunch and play poker or rummy or something. We've got a deck of cards."

Kelsey thought fast. No way would she be allowed to spend the whole day with a boy Mom hadn't met, especially if it meant leaving Kelsey behind with him while the family went off somewhere. "I'd like to," Kelsey said carefully to Herb, "but usually my family goes to the ocean beach in the afternoon, and I don't think they'd – "

"Right," Herb said. "Well, Gabe's been after me to try an ocean beach, but I'm too lazy to climb up and down those steep cliffs." He turned to his son. "How about cadging a ride with Kelsey's party, Gabe?"

Gabe looked embarrassed. "Hey, Dad!" he said.

"Gabe thinks I'm pushy," Herb said to Kelsey. "He's stuffy like his mother. Tell you what, I could drop him off at whatever beach you're going to, and he could hang out there with you."

"I'm sure my father would be happy to give him a ride," Kelsey hastened to say. She was so concerned not to have Gabe thinking that she didn't want him that she forgot about keeping him away from her family. For the crucial moment she forgot. Then, too late, she remembered and bit her lip.

"Thanks," Gabe said, accepting her offer. "How about if I come by your cottage, and if it's okay – "

"Oh, it'll be fine. Come around one. It'll take them that long to get going." What else could she say? Now she'd done it!

"And I'll have a peaceful snooze while you're gone," Herb said.

Kelsey dragged herself home. This afternoon Gabe would meet her family. This afternoon he would learn her age, and who knew what else. There was no hope. No help. Her big romance was kaput.

They were all in the living room. Dad was eating. Mom was reading yesterday's local paper. Ria was doing stretching exercises, and Sara was cutting out paper dolls, yet another new toy. The diary was where Kelsey had left it, but that didn't necessarily mean it hadn't been read.

"Umm," she began. "I told Gabe he could get a ride to the beach with us this afternoon. You said you wanted to meet him." She felt limp. She sounded limp.

"Good," Mom said complacently. "When's he coming?"

Ria stared wide-eyed at Kelsey as she answered her mother.

"You *invited* him?" Ria asked her later when they were alone on the deck.

"It sort of popped out of me. Ria, couldn't I be like

74 ·

nine months younger than you instead of two years?"

"How are you going to manage that with Mom and Dad around?"

Kelsey whimpered. "I'll start choking if anyone mentions age, and you whack me on the back, and then I can pinch Sara, and she'll howl, and maybe you can faint or something."

"You're crazy," Ria said. "I think you're really off the wall nuts."

She was, Kelsey thought. Positively nuts. She should have run away from home or drowned herself instead of walking right into the disaster this afternoon was going to be. But meanwhile, she still had the ten o'clock swim. Her last time alone with Gabe. She wore the new swimsuit Mom had bought her before the budget crunched. It was blue but it did make her legs look very long.

"Was Mother with you when you bought that?" Ria asked, looking at Kelsey's chest.

"Sure. Can't you see it's blue? But I've probably developed since May. Don't look at me, Ria. It's embarrassing. Do I look gross?"

"You look sexy." Ria considered. "And older than you are. Maybe you'll get away with it after all."

"Get away with what?" Sara asked from the doorway. She was enveloped in Mom's hooded sweatshirt except for two plump bare legs and two big brown eyes.

"Nothing," Kelsey said. She advanced threateningly on her little sister. "And if you dare to say anything to Gabe about me, anything at all this afternoon, I'll sneak into your bedroom while you're sleeping and rip First Turtle to bits." Snarling, Kelsey made claws of her hands and reached toward Sara.

"Maaaaa!" Sara yelled.

"I haven't even touched you," Kelsey said.

"Your friend's here, Kelsey," Mom called from the front door.

"Oh, my God! What's he doing to me?" Kelsey leaped onto the bed and hid her head under the covers.

"Stop acting like a baby," Ria hissed. "Come on. Get up."

"Why are you always so mean to me, Kelsey?" Sara whined. "All's I did was ask a question."

"She was just kidding. Weren't you, Kelsey?" Ria said. "She's sorry, Sara."

"No, I'm not." Kelsey stood, tugged her suit up, threw the first T-shirt that came to hand on over it, and marched out to Gabe who was chatting in the kitchen with Mother.

"You're welcome to have lunch with us too," Mom was saying to him sweetly. No doubt what kind of impression he'd made on her.

"Thanks, Mrs. Morris," he said, "but if I'm going to desert my dad for most of the day, I'd better eat lunch with him. . . . Is it okay if Kelsey and I take a quick swim in the bay now?"

They went for a long, vigorous swim. Coming out of the water, Gabe said, "You looked as if you could have kept going clear to Great Island." He was smiling admiringly.

"Not that far."

"But you're a really strong swimmer. You're like a porpoise in the water."

His smile and the compliment were doing strange things to her. "Why did you come to the house instead of meeting me on the beach?" she blurted out.

He frowned. "Wasn't that all right? I didn't want to miss you again."

"Oh," she said, and scarcely able to breathe, she added, "See you after lunch?"

"Right. I'll be over at one." He collected his towel from the concrete retaining wall where she'd left her shirt, and slung it around his neck. Water was still dripping off his hair. His cheeks were burnished from the sun. She would have liked to tell him how handsome he was but was afraid of not being cool. Instead she swiped his towel and ran.

He chased her shouting, "Hey, that's mine."

When he'd retrieved the towel, she asked him, "Does it make you mad to be teased?"

"No ... I guess I like it ... I don't get teased much."

"Poor Gabe," she said and left before she melted altogether.

The morning had been so wonderful. What would the afternoon bring? If only the parents didn't mention her age, and if only Sara turned dumb, and if only Gabe didn't fall madly in love with Ria – if only none of those things happened, the afternoon might pass without doom and disaster. Maybe.

7

It started out okay. The conversation between Gabe and her parents seemed harmless, and Kelsey wasn't part of it. She sat between Gabe and Ria in the rear seat of the station wagon contemplating the back of Sara's head which was sleek and dark as a seal's. How nice if Sara *were* a cute, mute pet seal, Kelsey thought.

"You've never been to Wellfleet before?" Dad asked Gabe over his shoulder. They were waiting for the traffic to allow them to cross Route 6 and continue toward the ocean side, three miles away from the bay at this narrow end of the Cape.

"My mother tells me I was here when I was two, but I don't remember. . . . From what I've seen so far, I'd say it's a great place."

"Yes, we love it. The ocean beaches can't be beat for my money," Dad said. "You can walk the shore all the way to P-town or as many miles in the other direction."

"Yeah, I noticed that when I looked at the map," Gabe said, "but my Dad can't be pried loose from the bay."

"You and your father are here alone?" Mother asked.

"Right. My parents are divorced. Kelsey probably told you that this is a first — me spending time with my father."

"Kelsey never tells us anything," Mother said.

"Mom!" Kelsey protested. "That's not fair."

"Relax. I'm just kidding," Mom said.

Kelsey knew better, and she couldn't relax. Any second Mom was likely to mention the awfulness of thirteen year olds, or Sara would get in the conversation and say she was only seven and Kelsey was six years older.

"What part of the country are you from, Gabe?" Dad wanted to know.

"Albany, New York. My mother teaches chemistry at the state university there."

"Are you an only child?" Mom asked, steering back into the personal.

"Is it that obvious?" Gabe said in dismay.

"Well, you're comfortable talking to adults, like many only children. I'm sure Kelsey envies you."

Kelsey slid lower in her seat, gritting her teeth over her mother's casual disregard for her privacy. Mom guarded her own. Yet she never hesitated to expose her children to public view, especially her middle child, as if she were a bare-bottomed infant.

"Kelsey's the one to be envied," Gabe said, squeezing her hand reassuringly. "Being an only child's boring."

Sara's big eyes suddenly appeared over the top of

the front seat. "I wish *I* had a big brother," she said.

"How come?" Gabe asked her with a grin.

"Well, because." Sara flirted with him shamelessly. "Because they might be nice and play with me."

"We play with you, Sara," Ria said.

"*You* do sometimes, but not Kelsey. She hates me." With that, Sara sank out of sight.

Kelsey groaned and vowed to herself never again to let loose her family on a new friend. Never ever ever. Thanks to Mom and Sara, Gabe must think she was some kind of witch girl.

Finally, to Kelsey's relief, they made it into the Newcomb Hollow Beach parking lot.

Ria was in the lead. She asked, "Left or right when we get down to the beach?"

"Either way," Dad said. He hefted the two heavy beach chairs.

"Left looks emptier," Mom said. She was carrying the beach towels and her sun hat and a book. Ria had the insulated bag with the lemonade and cookies. Gabe took the umbrella, and Kelsey carried the paddle-ball game and bag with the sunscreen and miscellaneous essentials like tissues. She was biding her time until they'd settled someplace. Then she would try to get Gabe away from the family somehow.

As usual, for safety's sake, they went no farther then the red flag that marked the end of the lifeguard's domain. Ahead of them the beach was bare and inviting.

"Let's keep going to where there's more room, Gabe," Kelsey said to him softly.

"This is fine here."

"I mean, we don't have to stay with the family," she explained.

"Why?" he looked confused. "Don't you want to?"

"I just thought maybe you might be sick of all the questions."

"No problem. They're just being parents. Next they'll check out what kind of student I am."

"You've got it," Kelsey agreed and urged, "let's take off before they start."

His eyes twinkled. "Not to worry. I'll pass the test."

The ocean was calm, so flat that Kelsey began apologizing for it. "I don't know what happened to the waves. Usually there's lots of them to ride and plenty of surf, too."

"Looks like good swimming," Gabe said. He turned to Kelsey's mother and asked politely, "Mind if we go in now?"

"Enjoy," she said with a dismissive wave of her hand.

Without checking to see if Kelsey or her sisters would follow him, he dropped the beach umbrella and his towel and sprinted for the water yelling, "Last one in's a chicken head."

Kelsey followed right on the heels of his shallow dive and came up beside him. "Yeow, it's cold," he complained.

"It's colder than the bay," she admitted, "but the water's clearer here, and it's fun to jump waves — when there are waves."

They came out shivering, wrapped themselves in

beach towels, and joined Ria on an old bedspread where she was idly sifting sand through her fingers. Mom was in her chair, immersed in a book. Dad was building a sand castle with Sara in the wet sand near the water.

"Kelsey says you're the athlete," Gabe said to Ria.

"She's a better swimmer than I am," Ria said.

"Ria's got a shelf full of tennis trophies," Kelsey boasted. "She would have gone to tennis camp this summer if Dad hadn't – " Kelsey caught herself on the edge of Dad's sore spot and glanced his way. Luckily he didn't seem to be listening.

"I thought I was a pretty good tennis player until I tried out for my high school team and decided I'd better stick to running," Gabe said.

Kelsey listened, alert for any age-revealing conversation. At the first sign of any, she'd divert him – like she'd scream that something had bitten her and go dashing into the ocean again, or she'd jump up and say, "look," and point to the sky.

The pock, pock, pock rhythm of the father-son paddle-ball game next to them gave her the idea for how to keep Gabe active and off dangerous conversational ground. She got out the paddles and plum-sized ball and asked, "Who wants to play?"

"Why don't you and Ria show me how it's done," Gabe suggested.

"Ria's the champ," Kelsey said.

"Don't be silly," Ria said. "You're just as good."

Because Gabe was watching, Kelsey concentrated hard on getting the ball back. She leaped, and lunged from side to side, smacking the ball smartly with the light wooden paddle. As they exceeded their all time total of forty-eight hits in a row, Ria got excited and began counting aloud. At sixty-four Kelsey missed. Gabe clapped. "You're both super," he said.

"Come on." Ria offered him her paddle. "Try it."

"I'm pooped," Kelsey said. "You and Gabe hit and I'll watch. Please, Ria."

He missed at first, but he kept trying, unselfconscious even though they were watching him. Even Mother was watching over the top of her book. "Nice boy," she murmured to Kelsey. "But he's a little old for you, isn't he?"

"No, he's *not*." Kelsey's heart beat double time in alarm.

"He looks at least sixteen, maybe seventeen."

Kelsey hesitated. Tell Mom or let her ask Gabe? Best to tell. "He's fifteen, and two years is no big deal, Mom. It's not like he's a man and I'm a little girl or something."

"Just be careful you don't get in trouble pretending to more sophistication than you have."

"I'm more sophisticated than you think. I'm just as sophisticated as Ria."

"That's not saying much," Mom said. "She's too busy with sports to have paid any attention to boys yet."

Kelsey chewed on her lip to keep from telling Mom she didn't know her eldest daughter as well as she thought. Ria had been having quiet crushes on boys since fifth grade. True, she didn't have the boyfriend

Kelsey had told Gabe about, but Ria *had* been holding hands with a boy in the halls of the high school in May. A locker love, Ria'd called it, because she never got as far as going out with him after school. "Don't tell Mom or Dad," Ria had said, and of course, Kelsey hadn't.

"That game's more fun than it looks," Gabe said. His bronzed skin was glistening as he dropped onto the spread.

"There's lemonade in the thermos if you're thirsty," Mom offered.

"No, thanks."

"We could take a walk," Kelsey suggested hopefully, still angling to keep him out of the range of age-related questions.

"Give the boy a chance to rest," Mom chided her. She smiled at Gabe. "Are you involved in any school sports, Gabe?"

"Not really. I run some, but I'm carrying three honors courses, and I tutor a kid in math pretty regularly. That uses up most of my time."

"Three honors courses," Mother said. "You must be an excellent student."

"I do okay. At least in science and math."

"That's nice to hear," Mom, the math teacher, said. She retired into her book, obviously satisfied with the answers Gabe had given. His predictions were so correct that Kelsey tried to repress a giggle. Gabe heard it and started laughing.

"What did I say?" Mom asked. "I didn't mean to be funny."

"You weren't," Gabe said. "We're just being silly."

"You were giving Gabe the third degree," Ria said.

"Certainly not. I was just trying to get to know him. What's wrong with that?"

"Nothing," Gabe assured her.

They were quiet then. Gabe put his head down on his arms and closed his eyes which allowed Kelsey to relax and watch him unobserved. She liked the hollowed-out depths of his eye sockets and the way his cheekbones jutted. His legs were surprisingly hairy, but his dark head shone in the sunlight. Best of all was the way he had opened himself up to her when they were alone, as if he trusted her, as if she were someone special.

"He's cute," Ria whispered.

"But he's mine," Kelsey reminded her quickly.

Sara appeared, legs coated with sand and suit straps dangling. She crouched next to Gabe and coaxed, "We really need your help, Daddy and me. This is the neatest sand castle ever."

"Sure." Gabe got up. Determined to monitor his conversations with her family, Kelsey got up too and helped work on the sand castle. It did look impressive with four towers, a moat, a road, and a series of stepped battlements.

"Not bad, huh?" Dad said with pride when they were finished.

"And there's no waves to knock it down, either," Sara said.

"The tide will take it tonight after we're gone," Dad told her.

"Oh, no!" Sara cried.

"But that's good," Gabe told her. "Then you can have the fun of building another one tomorrow."

"I don't want to build another one," Sara said firmly.

"Gabe's right, Sara," Dad said. "The fun's in the doing, not the having." He smiled at Kelsey. "Like the drawings Kelsey used to ball up and throw away after she worked so hard on them."

"I wouldn't have thrown them away if they had been any good," Kelsey said.

"You're an artist?" Gabe asked her.

"No."

"She could be," Dad said. "She won a prize for her school at an art contest in the mall last year."

"Oh, Dad, that was no big deal."

"Don't you take credit for anything?" Gabe asked her.

"Sure I do."

"For what then?" he challenged her.

"I told you I could swim."

"And that's it? You're no good at anything else?" He was teasing her, she saw.

"Let's go for a walk," she said again. "We have time, Dad, don't we?"

"Sure. We won't leave for another hour or so." Dad went to his chair and picked up a magazine.

"I'll walk too," Sara said, not to Kelsey but to Gabe.

"You aren't invited," Kelsey said, and added in case

Gabe thought she was being too mean, "I want to talk to Gabe about some things."

"What things?" Sara asked.

"We'll see you in a little while," Gabe told her firmly.

Sara stood watching them go for a minute before turning back to the rest of the family.

"She's such a pest," Kelsey said.

"I think she's kind of cute," Gabe said.

"Well, you don't have to live with her."

"I like your family," Gabe said. "They're all nice in their own way."

"My father's the best," Kelsey said. "Most of my friends wish he was their father because he's fun. Well, he was. This summer he's been down a lot because he's worried about getting another job as good as the one he had. He was a manager of engineering, and it really wasn't his fault his company went out of business. But I wish we could have stayed in Cincinnati. I still can't believe I'm not going back to school there next fall."

"You're a daddy's girl, aren't you?"

"I used to be before Sara was born. At least, Mom says I was. But now Sara's Daddy's girl . . . Ria's closest to Mom."

"Where does that leave you?"

"Me? I'm the lump in the middle."

"You're no lump," he said. "How come you put yourself down so much?"

"I don't. It's just when I'm with my family because

— well, Ria's pretty nearly perfect, and she's got the straight blond hair, and she's cool. And my rotten little sister's so cute. You said it yourself."

"Not as cute as you, though."

Delighted at the unexpected compliment, Kelsey nevertheless opened her mouth to object. Then she didn't. If he thought she was cute, it would be foolish to talk him out of it. She studied him out of the corner of her eyes. Was he teasing her? He looked perfectly serious. "I'm the one everybody fights with," she said.

"How come?" He bent to pick up a seagull feather and presented it to her. She took it gravely and stuck it in her hair.

"I don't know. That's just the way it is . . . Because I don't fit."

He shook his head. "Family relationships are a mystery to me. It's probably a good thing I only have to deal with my mother most of the time."

She was thinking that his father was likable, too. "I bet if we could get your dad here, he'd change his mind about the ocean beach," she said.

"He says the dunes are too steep for him. He doesn't have much energy. I asked him if he's feeling all right, and he says he's fine, just that he's a couch potato. Maybe he's lazy. I guess lots of people think vacation's for lying around and catching up on their sleep."

"Not me. I hate sitting still."

"Yeah, you're a high energy type."

"Is that bad?"

"Good." He smiled at her.

Another compliment to stow away until she was alone and could take it out with his others to wear like jewelry. She'd preen with them in front of the mirror where no one could see to mock her.

Gabe's eyes followed the high dunes looming above them. "This is a lot more rugged than the Jersey shore, a lot more beautiful, too."

"You should see the sky over the ocean on a stormy day. That's really awesome."

"Well, if we get a storm, we'll come and watch. Okay?"

"We could hitchhike over," she said.

"Better to rent bikes."

"No money," she said. She'd spent her savings on gifts for her friends before she'd left Cincinnati.

"My treat." He took her hand. The only people in sight were a couple sleeping on a blanket in each other's arms, and in the distance a man fishing in the surf. Gabe tugged her slightly toward him.

He was planning to kiss her, Kelsey realized. She drew away, blurting out, "We'd better go back. They're probably waiting for us."

He dropped her hand. "Sure," he said.

Immediately, she began worrying that he was angry at her for pulling back. She would have liked to kiss him. It had to be different from being swiped on the ear by a seventh-grade boy. Kissing Gabe by the ocean would be romantic. Then why had she stopped him? Scared, she accused herself. Yes, she was scared. She might not do it right. And what about after they kissed, what happened then? She drank and smoked, she'd told him. What else would he expect? His being older complicated things.

She was quiet walking back, busy sliding about in all her uncertainties. Gabe wasn't saying anything either. Had she blown it by not letting him kiss her? Maybe now he didn't think she was cute or full of energy or a good swimmer or anything. Kiss me, she wanted to yell, but she couldn't open her mouth.

Kelsey and Gabe helped the others gather up the beach paraphernalia, and they climbed back up the dune single file. In the parking lot, Dad stopped to admire a motorcycle. "Looks just like the one I had when I was sixteen."

"Sixteen?" Gabe stopped beside him. "Your folks let you have a motorcycle when you were only sixteen?"

"Well, we lived in the country, so traffic wasn't a problem."

"Boy, I'd love a motorcycle. I'll be sixteen next spring, but my mother's never going to believe that's old enough."

"So you're fifteen?" Dad said. "Same age as Ria."

"And Kelsey," Gabe said.

"Kelsey's thirteen," Dad said casually. He gave the motorcycle a fond last look before going to unlock the trunk of the car.

Kelsey ducked her head to avoid Gabe's stare. He didn't say anything, and she didn't look up. The silence burned right down to her toes. She barely had the strength to get in the car, and she stared at her knees all the way home, careful not to let her body touch his. She had been so sure it would be Sara or Mom who'd tell. She had been so wrong.

Dad was talking about a television special they ought to watch that evening.

"We don't have a TV at our rental," Gabe said.

"Come watch on ours," Dad said. "It's supposed to be an excellent production if you're interested in the Civil War at all."

"Oh, I am. I'm a Civil War buff," Gabe said. "Well, sort of. I have a Confederate flag, and a hat from a Union officer's uniform on the wall of my bedroom."

"We'll expect you at eight then," Dad said.

Kelsey's first reaction was amazement that learning how old she was hadn't put Gabe off, that he was coming over to watch TV at her house as if everything was the same. Then she realized *why* he was coming. Of course; he liked her family. As Dad's TV buddy, Gabe could switch smoothly to the right age sister. Well, Kelsey wasn't going to witness it. No way. She would have a terrible headache and hide out in her room.

The only thing she really regretted was that she'd lied to his father. Could anything be worse? Not kissing Gabe was bad; lying about her sister was bad, but being thirteen and lying about it to his father – she wanted to die. She wanted to sink out of sight beneath her own foolishness. It was no wonder if Gabe would rather be Ria's friend.

8

Kelsey squeezed her misery into a ball and curled up around it on her bed. Ria found her crying when she came to change from bathing suit to shorts and T-shirt. "What's the matter with you?" she wanted to know.

"Didn't you hear Dad tell Gabe?"

"Tell him what?"

Kelsey rubbed her wet eyes with the top of the sheet. "Dad told him how old I am."

"Oh . . . So what did Gabe say?"

"Nothing."

"Nothing? But he's coming over tonight to watch a TV show? You're really lucky."

"You don't understand."

"What? He can't be mad at you if he knows and he's still coming . . . Right?"

"But now he thinks I'm just a little kid."

"Oh, well, at least you won't have to lie anymore," Ria said.

Before Kelsey could set Ria straight on Gabe's real reason for coming, Mom appeared. "What's wrong, Kelsey? Why are you in bed?"

"I'm just tired."

"You've been crying. Did that boy do something to you?"

"No! Of course not. I told you, Mom, it's nothing."

"You're hysterical about nothing?"

Kelsey yanked the pillow over her head to escape her mother's infuriating logic.

"What *is* the matter with her?" Mom asked Ria. "We all liked him, and he seemed to be having a good time. What's she upset about?"

"It's all right, Mom. I'll take care of it," Ria said.

As soon as she heard her mother walking away, Kelsey came up for air. "Thanks," she said. "You understand, Ria. Don't you?"

Ria shrugged. "Not really. I think it's better that everything's out in the open. This way he can hang out with us all you want."

Kelsey groaned. "Hang out with you, you mean. That's what he's going to want to do now."

"You're crazy," Ria said. "What gives you that idea? He never even looked at me."

"You'll see. Tonight when he comes, you'll see," Kelsey predicted in a voice of gloom.

Ria shrugged and went away. A few minutes later Dad appeared. "Ria says you're upset because I told Gabe your age. I didn't realize it was top secret, Kelsey. You should have warned me."

"It's okay, Dad." Bravely, she added, "I don't blame you."

"Good. Listen, he's a nice kid, and you can be friends with him anyway, even if – "

She interrupted him. "Go away, please. Just go away. . . ." She couldn't bear listening to another speech about friendship, even from him.

"Actually," Dad sounded miffed by her rejection, "it's your own fault for pretending to be older."

"I know it's my own fault. Everything's my fault. Now, please, leave me alone."

He went off muttering about girls getting emotional over nothing, but she didn't care. Why was it, she wondered, that when she wanted her family to notice her, they didn't, but just let her want to be alone, and they swarmed all over her.

A while later Ria came to call her to supper. "I'm not hungry," Kelsey said. "You can entertain Gabe tonight."

"No thanks. He's your friend. I wouldn't know what to say to him."

"He's easy to talk to," Kelsey advised her, but Ria walked off.

Kelsey had no doubt Ria would manage just fine with Gabe. Now that he wasn't the stranger he'd been to her this afternoon, she wouldn't be shy with him, especially in her own house. If Kelsey ventured into the living room this evening, Gabe would say carelessly, "Hi, kid," as if she were a child. Worse yet, if he asked why she'd lied about her age, what would she answer? What could she answer?

"Because I wanted you to like me," was the truth. He'd laugh like an indulgent big brother if she admitted that.

"Rats!" She punched her pillow. If only he'd known her a little longer before he found out her age, he might have overlooked it. She should have let him kiss her this afternoon. She should have proved her maturity by saying deep, wise, wonderful, memorable things. "You always give such good advice," Jennifer had often told her. And Cathy had once quoted something Kelsey had said to her as if it were something from "Dear Abby." But it was too late. She'd lost him.

All she could hope for was that someday when she was in her twenties and had a glamorous job as a TV newscaster or a journalist like Aunt Syl, she'd bump into Gabe in an airport. She'd be elegant in a long, slim, expensive outfit, and he'd stare at her and say, "Don't I know you?"

She'd look amused and toss her sleek, well-cut hair – auburn now instead of rusty. "Weren't you my sister's boyfriend one summer when we were kids on Cape Cod?" she'd ask. Or better yet, she'd pretend not to recognize him, and with the same amused look, she'd say coolly, "*That's* an old line," and keep walking. Except, what if he didn't follow? No, she'd just say her name, and then she'd say, "You liked my sister better than me that summer. Well, she has five children and her own tennis camp now." *Six* children maybe, and a husband, of course.

"I didn't like your sister better," he'd say. "But what could I do? You were only thirteen."

"Two years makes no difference."

"You're right. I don't know why I ever thought it

did," he'd say. Then he'd take her hand and pull her close to him. . . .

"Kelsey." It was Ria with Sara skulking behind her. "Listen, Mom says you should get up. She says to tell you you can have those shorts you wanted if that will make you feel better."

"What happened to the budget?"

"Dad says he can afford a pair of shorts. Come on, Kelsey."

With a catch in her voice, she told Ria, "Gabe was going to rent bikes so we could bike to the beach in a storm."

"What storm?" Sara asked, edging up close to peer down at Kelsey.

"If there was a storm."

"Oh," Sara said.

"Just act as if nothing happened, and I bet it'll work out fine with him," Ria said.

"It can't now that he thinks I'm a baby."

"Well, stop acting like one," Ria said impatiently.

"But Mama won't let you go to the beach in a storm, will she?" Sara asked, her nose inches from Kelsey's.

Kelsey sighed. "It doesn't matter now. He won't take me."

"Do you want to hold First Turtle for a while?" Sara asked. It was her ultimate offer of sympathy.

Kelsey was touched. "No, thanks, Sara." She patted Sara's arm.

"Listen," Ria said, "he'll be here any minute, and he'll think you're weird if you're still in your bathing suit."

That hit a nerve. Kelsey vaulted from her bed to the wall of drawers, grabbed some clothes and ran off to the bathroom. When she came out dressed in soft old jeans and a white sweatshirt, Gabe was sitting on the couch in the living room watching TV with the family.

As she'd expected, he barely noticed her. He and Dad had their eyes fixed on the screen. Mom was hemming a skirt. Sara was lying on the floor with her chin on her arms propped on First Turtle. Seeing them all there, with Gabe so comfortable in their midst, Kelsey felt the old glass wall between her and her family again, but now Gabe was on the other side of it with them. She was the outsider and he was the one who belonged.

The diary was still lying on the coffee table where she'd left it. If one of *them* had left a diary lying out in the open, she'd have read it. *She* was interested in their secret thoughts and feelings, but they didn't care enough about her to even be curious.

"There you are, Kelsey," Mom said. "Feeling better?"

"I'm fine." She smiled boldly at Gabe who had turned around to see her. "Want some popcorn?" she asked him as coolly as if having him there didn't faze her.

"Sure." Gabe returned his attention to the screen.

"I want some too," Sara said.

Kelsey shook the popcorn in the Dutch oven over a burner while she snacked on cold leftover spaghetti directly from the refrigerator. Just as the program Gabe had come to watch ended, she delivered a bowlful of warm buttered popcorn to the living room.

"Thanks," Gabe said and took a handful.

"Kelsey makes the best popcorn," Ria said.

"Kelsey's a good cook. When she feels like it," Mom said.

"But she doesn't put enough chocolate chips in her cookies," Sara said. "Dad makes the best chocolate chip cookies."

"Brownies are my specialty," Gabe said. "I tried to make some to bring over tonight, but the oven in our cabin doesn't work very well."

"Remember the brownies *you* had to bake for your class party, Ria?" Mom asked.

Ria laughed and, without any sign of shyness, told the story about the ten dozen brownies that she couldn't make when their oven quit working at just the wrong time. ". . . Then the supermarket was out of brownies when Mom took me there at the last minute. So we finally ended up buying doughnuts, which would have been okay, except when I got to school, it turned out I had the date wrong, too, and we were a week early."

"I remember those doughnuts," Dad said. "You stuck them in the freezer and we ate them for weeks."

"*You* did," Mom said. "You were the only one who liked them."

"No wonder they lasted so long!" Dad said.

"I think I'll go for a walk," Kelsey said and looked pointedly at Gabe.

"Now?" Mom asked.

"Just down to the beach to see the sunset."

"It's over."

"Not yet." Kelsey could see reddish clouds through the window above the tops of the pitch pines. She looked at Gabe again, but he kept on sitting there, mesmerized by the TV. "I'll be back soon," Kelsey said and fled.

She ran all the way to the beach. The sunset-watchers were heading home. All that was left was a purple shadow high above the outline of bluffs. The water was dead calm; its stillness soothed her. It had happened just as she expected. Gabe saw her as an awkward child now. He'd lost interest. And all she could do was try not to make a fool of herself by showing how grieved she was. It got darker. Her feet chilled.

She dragged back to the cottage into the glow of lamplight and the warmth of the family circle.

Gabe was still there. "Hi," he said. "Catch the sunset?"

"Umm."

They were watching a documentary on Alaska now. She sat down cautiously in a chair, turned so that she couldn't see the TV very well, but could keep her eyes on Gabe. Unobtrusively, she got her sketch pad and began working. So far all she'd done were dunes and a page of pebbles at low tide. What had appealed to her about the pebbles was their multicolored variety gleaming under water, and she hadn't been able to capture that with her pencil no matter how carefully she shaded. Still, she liked that picture.

She began to sketch Gabe's face. His oddly set eyes were his most distinctive feature, but they were harder to capture than his long, straight nose. That came out right the first time. She tried the eyes again.

"Sketching, Kelsey?" Mom asked during a commercial break.

"Just fooling around."

"Can I see?" Gabe asked.

"No." She closed the sketch pad fast.

"Kelsey's won prizes for her drawing," Ria said.

"So I've heard," Gabe said.

"I can draw too," Sara said. "Want to see the birthday card I made for Mommy?"

"Sure." He admired Sara's purple turtle card lavishly.

"Why won't you show Gabe your work, Kelsey?" Mom asked. "Since when are you so shy?"

"I'm not. It's just not worth showing." Kelsey got up and took the sketch pad to her bedroom.

She heard Dad ask, "Who's for ice cream? Gabe, how about you?"

"Sure," Gabe said.

She returned for the ice cream, her favorite Heath Bar Crunch. While they ate, they talked about the Civil War program they'd seen and how history was taught in high school. Ria said she liked being lectured to when the teacher was good. Gabe said reading original documents did it best for him. "You know, you read some letter about how a guy staked his claim in the Klondike and really get a feel for what the Gold Rush was like up there."

"Are you going to be a history teacher?" Ria asked.

"Not likely. It just interests me. A lot of things do."

"That's healthy," Dad said. "Around here everybody's a monomaniac. Ria's only interested in tennis, and Sara's only interested in turtles, and Kelsey – "

"*You're* only interested in food, Daddy," Sara interrupted him to say. They all laughed and let the subject drop. Kelsey was glad she'd escaped being tagged. What would Dad have said? Kelsey's only interested in herself? That's what Mother accused her of often enough.

In the kitchen, when she and Ria were washing the bowls and spoons, Ria whispered to her, "Kelsey, what's the matter with you? You know, you're acting as if you're mad at him. Relax."

"How can I relax in this family?"

"I think he likes us," Ria said. She looked over her shoulder across the open counter into the living room and added, "And some of us like him a lot."

Kelsey followed her gaze. Sara was leaning against Gabe, looking up adoringly, "Do you like turtles, Gabe?" she asked him.

A few minutes later he untangled himself from his youngest admirer and said he'd better be getting home.

"We'll be going to the ocean beach again tomorrow

probably," Dad said. "You're welcome to come along."

"Thanks," Gabe said. "But my dad wants to go down to Provincetown tomorrow."

"Good beach there at Race Point," Dad said.

Kelsey waited until he was out the door. Then she ran down the steps after his dark shape, catching up with him in the middle of the lane.

"Gabe," she said, glad she couldn't see him clearly.

"Kelsey? Is that you?"

"I have to know what you thought. I mean really. Were you mad when Dad told you how old I am?"

He hesitated. "My father explained it to me."

"He did? How?"

"He said, 'it's a woman's prerogative to lie about her age.'"

"Oh, I don't think so," Kelsey said. "Nobody has a right to lie about anything."

"So then how come you did?" She could hear a smile in his voice.

"Because I was afraid you wouldn't like me if you knew my real age," she blurted out, just as she'd feared she might. She caught her breath then and waited.

"Oh," he said finally. "Yeah. Well, okay." He hesitated. But all he added before he walked away was, "Okay, then. I'll see you."

"After Provincetown?" she called. "Will I see you?"

"I don't know how long we'll be. Maybe."

She stood there until his footsteps faded, and all she

could hear was her own heart beating. How could she have begged like that? Thirteen! She'd acted as childish as Sara. Pathetic to have so little dignity. If she saw him again, if she *ever* saw him again, she'd show him dignity. She'd be cool and distant and dignified as Mom, or Queen Elizabeth, or one of Sara's stupid, snaky-headed turtles.

9

Kelsey woke up feeling ugly. How was she going to project a cool, mature image considering what she had to project from? She waited until her parents were making breakfast, then sneaked into their room to survey herself in Aunt Syl's full-length mirror. The girl frowning from the mirror had a pert, freckled face and a wild mass of red hair. She looked intense, not cool.

Kelsey eliminated the frown, but that didn't help. Her body was slim enough, except that maybe her legs should be longer and her chest could stick out less. What she needed was clothes, an important top for the new yellow shorts Mother had promised her, something adult with a collar, tailored maybe. But it would be considered greedy to ask for that, too.

She'd pay for her own top if she were back in Cincinnati earning money baby-sitting, but here she couldn't earn money. Unless she put up a sign, SITTER AVAILABLE, and her phone number — on a pole near the beach would be good. Except, by the time she had the money, the month would be over and Gabe would be gone.

"There you are, Kelsey," Mom said from the doorway. "Your father's leaving for that job interview in Boston."

"What job interview?"

"You know that man you suggested he contact, Masden? Well, Dad called him and Mr. Masden connected him with someone in Boston."

"Oh, good." Kelsey was glad that an idea of hers had worked.

"It probably won't amount to anything," Mother said in haste to deflate her, "but anyway, I'm going along to see my old college roommate, Kay Winer. Do you want to come?"

"Is Ria going?"

"No, she's playing tennis this morning. We're dropping her at the courts. Sara doesn't want to go either, but we're making her."

"Why? I could baby-sit if you want."

"You would?" Mom's expression went from hopeful to doubtful. "I don't know. The way you and Sara fight, I'm afraid it wouldn't work out."

"That's insulting," Kelsey said, "really insulting, Mom. You won't let me take care of my own *sister*? Didn't Mrs. Ott tell you I was the best sitter she ever had? Why do you always have to put me down?"

Her mother eyed her speculatively. "Believe me, I'd rather not have to edit my conversation with Kay for Sara's ears ... What if I paid you something? Say half-price discount since she *is* your sister?"

"Fine. Terrific. I need money for a top to go with the shorts you're getting me."

Mom looked at the baggy shirt and faded shorts Kelsey had on. "Your wardrobe *is* pretty pathetic. Well, all right. Just let me check with Sara."

Kelsey turned back to the mirror. She put her hand on her hip and raised her eyebrows haughtily as she imagined herself decked out in a new outfit. She'd look at least sixteen. "It's how old you act, not how old you are that matters, Gabe," she'd tell him.

A squawk from Sara sent Kelsey running into the living room.

"What's the matter?"

"She'll beat me up, Mom," Sara was saying. Her cereal spoon dangled, forgotten between bowl and mouth.

"Sara Faith Morris, that's a rotten thing to say," Kelsey yelled. "When did I ever hit you?"

"But you pull my hair and pinch me, though."

"And I suppose you've always been a sweet little angel to me?"

Sara nodded emphatically. "Um hmm."

"Liar!" Kelsey shrieked. She appealed to her parents. "She's no angel. She really isn't, not to me." Tears filled her eyes at the injustice of it all.

"Forget it," Mom said wearily. "We haven't even started out the door, and you two are already fighting. It won't work, Kelsey. We'll take Sara along."

"But I want to stay and cut out my pictures," Sara whined.

Dad took over. "If you want to stay, Sara, you've got to promise to listen to your sister."

"Well, *she* should promise not to be mean," Sara said.

"Sara," Kelsey wheedled, trying out her new maturity. "You offered to let me use First Turtle yesterday, remember? I thought we were friends."

"That's 'cause I felt sorry for you."

"For what?" Mom asked.

"Because Gabe was mad at her, but then he wasn't."

Ria appeared with racquet and balls in hand to ask, "Are we ready to go?"

"Okay, Sara. You going or staying?" Mom wanted to know.

"Well," Sara said reluctantly, "I'll stay with Kelsey. But if she's mean to me, you better punish her when you get back."

"We won't pay her if she's mean . . . Fair enough?" Mom asked Kelsey.

Reluctantly, Kelsey nodded, even though it was outrageous to give Sara such power over her. Sara should be the one who had to behave. On the other hand, Kelsey intended to be a model sitter. If she could stay cool with Sara, it would be a cinch to convince Gabe of her maturity.

"Good luck, Dad." Kelsey kissed her father. "I hope this is the one you want."

"Thanks, honey." Dad kissed her back affectionately.

"Good luck to *you*, kid," Ria whispered to her before following the parents to the car. They were dressed for the city. Dad had on a tie, and Mom was wearing heels and earrings.

Sara helped Kelsey clear the breakfast dishes, but when Kelsey started washing them, she didn't stay to dry. "Aren't you going to help me?" Kelsey asked.

"I don't have to. You're getting paid."

Kelsey gritted her teeth, and began multiplying sevens until she'd calmed down. It was a trick Mom had suggested when Kelsey was Sara's age, and counting to ten had no effect on her temper. Having finished the dishes, Kelsey found Sara cutting pictures of animals out of a stack of nature magazines.

"Okay. Let's go to the beach now, Sara."

"I don't want to."

"Why not? It's a perfectly gorgeous beach day. It'd be a shame to waste it."

"I don't like that beach. I like the pond."

"Well, we can't get to the pond without a car, can we?"

"You could help me cut out pictures."

"Did Mom give you permission to cut up those magazines?"

"Aunt Syl left them for me. I'm going to make them into an animal book for my new teacher."

"You'd better write captions or a story to go with the pictures," Kelsey advised. "Just pasting them up won't impress a teacher."

"Yes, it will. I'm going to make a really nice cover."

"But that's stupid, Sara."

Sara's eyes filled and Kelsey's spirits sank. Still, she coaxed, "Look, you can cut and paste anytime — in the rain, in the evening. Let's do something outside while it's sunny."

"Like what?"

"Well, if you don't want the beach, we could go for a hike."

"I hate hiking."

"Want to spray each other with water from Aunt Syl's garden hose?"

Sara shook her head stubbornly. She picked up a picture of a squirrel and began cutting.

"Umm. How about berry picking? July's when blueberries ripen around here. I think."

"Blueberries?"

"Right. We could get a whole potful and make a pie or muffins or something."

"Later," Sara said.

Cool, Kelsey told herself, keep cool. Think like an iceberg. She was proud of how calmly she rose, found her sketch pad, and retired to the deck. A pair of round, cheeky chickadees were clinging to the bird-feeder in the pine tree that overhung the deck. Kelsey sat down and started sketching. She was absorbed in capturing the black and white head of a cute little upside-down gray-winged fellow when Sara appeared.

"I'm ready now."

"For what?"

"To pick the blueberries."

Kelsey was tempted to say, "Well, now you can wait for me," but she restrained herself. "Okay, let's go," she said cheerfully instead. She dropped her sketch pad and picked up a sand pail from the litter of beach equipment at the front of the wraparound deck. They started off down the sand lane. It crossed Kelsey's mind that the rubber thongs and shorts she and Sara had on were not ideal for foraging through ankle high bearberry patches in pitch pine and scrub oak woods. But turning back now would just give Sara another excuse to be difficult.

"Where are we going?" Sara asked.

"You know, along the road," Kelsey said vaguely.

"Is it far?"

Now that Kelsey thought about it, she recalled that Aunt Syl had taken them somewhere in the car for berry picking. They'd stopped along a stretch of road that had no houses. Still, the vegetation here looked so similar. There had to be blueberry bushes lurking nearby. "Not far," Kelsey said.

Sara stopped to pet a cat in a driveway. Two boys drove by in a pickup truck and one whistled at Kelsey. She was flattered, but glad they hadn't scared her by slowing down. Too bad Gabe and his father hadn't invited her to go to Provincetown with them. Mom said P-town was tacky, but Kelsey enjoyed all the weirdly costumed people parading along the waterfront street. She liked the fudge and taffy smells from the candy shops, and the pocket gardens where asters and cosmos and daisies bloomed. Best of all were the serious-looking commercial fishing boats on the long wharf.

They hadn't gone a quarter of a mile to the first patch of open woodland before Sara began to complain. "It's too far. I don't like to walk so far, Kelsey. Let's go back now."

"Don't you want to bring back berries? Anyway, you need the exercise. Walking's good for you."

Hopefully, Kelsey set off across the spongy mat of a bearberry patch up into woods at the corner of the road. No signs warned them to keep out, but, as Sara pointed out immediately, there weren't any paths encouraging them to enter, either.

"Just follow me," Kelsey said.

For a while Sara followed obediently. Then she demanded, "Where are the blueberries?"

"We're getting to them." At the top of the hill was a spot with few trees and high brush. Kelsey hoped some of that tangle was blueberry laden. The going got harder with more prickery plants and vines to catch at their bare legs. All at once Sara screamed.

"What's the matter?"

"Something bit me."

"Nothing bit you."

"Yes, it did. I'm bleeding."

Kelsey examined Sara's leg. "Just a little scratch," she said. "Don't be a baby, Sara."

"There's snakes in here. I know there is," Sara said fearfully.

"They'll run when they hear you coming."

"Snakes don't run." Sara set her mouth primly.

"They'll crawl away then," Kelsey said agreeably. "Come on, Sara. Exploring is fun. Isn't it pretty up here?"

"No."

"You can see the marsh if you look down that way through the trees."

"I don't want to. I want to go home."

"Soon as we pick the blueberries, we'll go."

But if there were blueberry bushes, Kelsey couldn't find them. She saw chalky, blue-gray bayberry used to scent candles, and more green-leaved plants than she could identify, crowded between the occasional pitch pine and scrub oak. "You want to stay here and I'll explore a little on my own?" Kelsey said.

"Don't leave me!" Sara begged.

"All right, all right. We'll go back down the hill on this side, and look for berries."

Just then a bee flew near Sara, and she lapsed into hysteria. Kelsey shooed the bee away with her bare hand and told Sara to stop being silly. Sara's shrill wailing was getting on Kelsey's nerves.

"Shut up," she said. "We'll go straight home down this hill." Finally, Sara subsided into an irritating whimper. As if the bee had really stung her, Kelsey thought. They set off again with Kelsey muttering to herself, "Cool. Cool. Cool," against the simmering heat of her anger.

At the bottom of the hill, the road was rimmed with poison ivy. Kelsey saw it with alarm. Sara had gotten a bad case of poison ivy a year ago and now detoured widely around any cluster of shiny leaves. "Leaflets three, leave them be," Dad had taught her, and Sara was a careful counter.

Kelsey was trying to scout a way past the dreaded

stuff when Sara suddenly realized what lay ahead. She screeched so piercingly that Kelsey put her hands over her ears to protect them.

"Stop that," she said. "Stop it, Sara." She raised her hand threateningly. Sara ducked and covered her head with her arms. Kelsey dropped her hand, shocked by the sudden rise of her own temper. Clobbering Sara wasn't going to win her any model baby-sitter awards.

"Relax," Kelsey said through gritted teeth. "I'll get you safely through to the road. I promise."

"Don't hit me," Sara said from under her arms.

"I'm not hitting you. Don't be stupid."

"You're mean, Kelsey. You're always mean to me."

Kelsey was so tempted to tell Sara what a bratty baby she was that she had to clamp her mouth shut to keep the words in. Cool, cool, cool, but she'd never felt as hot. She wanted to kill her sister who squealed and complained all the way past the poison ivy banks. Finally, they made it back to the road.

Only, Kelsey wasn't sure which road. They'd come down the other side of the hill. She tried to reason about the correct turn, but nothing looked familiar. This might be the marshy cove in front of Aunt Syl's house, but it might not be. Marshes poked grassy fingers in and around every twist in the roads in this area.

Kelsey couldn't admit her confusion to Sara. Instead, she set off to the left as if she were sure that was the way. When they got to a dead end, marked by a heap of smelly clamshells buzzing with green-headed flies, Sara caught on that they were lost.

"Where are we?" she asked reproachfully.

"It's okay," Kelsey said. "We just should have gone right."

"But I'm tired," Sara said.

"It can't be that far to get home."

It was though. It was amazingly far in the noonday sun, so far that Sara stopped whining and dragged silently along like an exhausted puppy. Their legs were scratched and bloody. Sara's face was dirt- and tear-streaked. Even Kelsey got tired.

She suggested it would be nice to wash off in the sun-warmed water from the outside hose, but Sara said no and limped past her into the relative cool of the cottage. She drank a glass of water and went to lie down. Kelsey was pouring herself a glass of juice when she noticed the note from Ria on the refrigerator. She read it twice before she believed it. If the blueberry hike had been a disaster, this was worse.

"Went for a walk on the beach with Gabe. Be back soon, Ria."

Hadn't he gone to P-town then? And what had happened to Ria's tennis? The woman she was supposed to play against had promised to drop her back at the cottage. Kelsey looked at the clock. Twelve ten. She and Sara had been lost for hours. What a miserable day. What a miserable, horrible, dud of a day.

She imagined Gabe and Ria on the beach together. Blond and dark, both tall and lean. Ria was probably even strong enough to handle the Windsurfer if she wanted. They could play tennis together. They had high school in common and who knew what else once they started talking.

Ria was even-tempered and sensible. What did Gabe need with a frizzy redhead who couldn't even find a blueberry without getting lost? Cool? She'd never be. She couldn't even pretend to be. She was stupid, awkward, and ugly. She was thirteen and she'd lost Gabe. No doubt about it.

10

Kelsey got the windup alarm clock from her parents' bedroom, set it on the coffee table and sat cross-legged on the floor to watch time pass. Fifteen minutes later she was still waiting, hugging her knees and rocking in time to the clock's tick.

In her mind, she saw Gabe and Ria walking on the beach, confiding their innermost secrets to each other. Ria was describing her feelings that time she'd won the trophy when she'd beaten her old rival in a tiebreaker and been hugged by the coach she'd never managed to please before. Gabe was talking about his relationship to his father, or maybe he was saying something admiring about girls who were good athletes and had long, straight blond hair.

Absorbed in her imaginings, Kelsey didn't even hear Sara come into the living room. Sara gave her a wary look, and silently picked up her cut and paste activity. Soon the snip snip of her scissors made a duet with the ticking.

The slower the minutes passed, the more angry Kelsey got. She'd always admired Ria's standards of right behavior. Hadn't Ria, as eldest, accepted the blame for the trampled tulips when they'd cut through the neighbor's garden? And Ria had walked to school every day in seventh grade because the bus driver had kicked a friend of hers off for something she hadn't done. Yet that same high-principled girl had just turned traitor and stolen her younger sister's boyfriend. Incredible!

The instant Ria sauntered in at two o' clock, Kelsey burst out, "How could you?"

"How could I what?"

"Go off with him alone like that. I *told* you how much I like him."

"Don't be crazy, Kelsey. What happened was, Gabe came looking for you, and you weren't here. So he asked me to go for a walk with him, and he looked sort of upset. So I went, but I didn't know what to say. We just walked."

"That's it?"

"That's it."

"Kelsey took me through poison ivy. I'm going to be a mess," Sara announced while Kelsey was taking a deep breath of relief.

"Poison ivy?" Ria asked.

"But what's wrong with Gabe?" Kelsey wanted to know. "What happened to him?"

"I don't know. Something about his father."

"Well, what? Didn't you ask him?"

"Ask him? I was doing my best to keep him from telling me. You know I'm not good at that kind of stuff."

"And she got us lost and we didn't find a single blueberry," Sara said.

Kelsey whipped around to confront Sara. "I got you home, didn't I? And I *didn't* take you through poison ivy."

Sara turned her back on Kelsey and said to Ria, "I don't think Mom should pay her, do you? Because she didn't take care of me and got me in poison ivy and let a bee nearly sting me."

"Sara, shut up," Kelsey said.

"That's rude. You're rude, Kelsey," Sara said. She turned toward Ria. "Isn't she rude to say 'shut up' to me?"

"Did you scrub yourself with soap and water where the poison ivy touched?" Ria asked her.

"Ria!" Kelsey yelled, "we weren't *in* poison ivy. She just saw some and got hysterical."

"Oh." Ria nodded. "So what are you doing now, Sara?"

"Making a book for school so my teacher will think I'm smart."

"Really? I guess Kelsey was a good baby-sitter then."

"Why?" Sara sounded startled.

"She got you home, and you're doing this nice project, right? So you'll tell Mom she did a good job, won't you?"

Sara looked at Kelsey doubtfully, and then at Ria. "Welllll . . . but – "

"Nice people don't try to get other people into

trouble," Kelsey said. "Nice, kind, *good* people try to make things work out right for their sisters."

Ria nodded emphatically, staring at Sara who dropped her eyes and busied herself with the paste-ups.

"Gabe's probably still on the beach if you want to talk to him," Ria said.

"Do you think he might need me?"

"I don't know. He was uptight, and you're good with emotional stuff."

That was true, Kelsey thought. She was good at feelings if nothing else. And what was wrong with Gabe anyway? Giving Ria a quick hug, Kelsey said, "Thanks."

"For what?"

"For being *for* me," Kelsey said in a shaky voice. She cast a look Sara's way. "No one else in this family is."

Kelsey took the shortcut across Aunt Syl's wooded backyard to the hot asphalt road, and then past a few cottages to the beach entrance, which was lined with parked cars.

The bay looked like green ice glittering in the still afternoon, especially past the shallows where mommies and daddies stood around in knee-deep water supervising their offspring. It didn't surprise Kelsey not to see Gabe in that crowd. He was more likely to be down by the jetty where the beach was wider. Had he had a fight with his father? Was that what was bothering him? Or maybe his father had told him something awful, like about why he'd left his wife. Whatever – she'd lend a sympathetic ear.

She kept pace for a while with a red-and-white striped Sunfish beating into the wind parallel to shore. And there, sure enough, was Gabe's lean back on one of the boulders that formed the breakwater. He was facing away from her toward the town of Wellfleet across the harbor.

She said his name as she climbed onto a pebbly pink granite rock behind the smooth greenish one on which he sat.

When he turned, she saw how tight with pain his face was and she asked, "Do you want to talk or be left alone?"

"I sure need to talk to someone," he said. "I tried calling my mother, but I couldn't get hold of her. I even tried bending your sister's ear, but she put me off." He swallowed. "God, I'm confused."

"Is it your father?"

"Yeah. I'm so mad at him I could spit. Why did he have to get into my life? He had no right when all he wanted – It's like he cheated me because – It's like he just wanted me to care about him so that he'd have someone to remember after he – "

She put a calming hand on his shoulder. "After he what? What did he do?"

"It's not what he did. It's what he's going to do. He's going to die, Kelsey. He's going to *die*."

She gasped.

"Yeah. That's a shocker, isn't it? And he's apologizing because he thought he'd have a whole year to live. The doctors told him – but as soon as we got here, he realized how weak he is. So he's apologizing like it matters that it's less than a year. I mean, as if *that's* the problem, not the whole – " Gabe gestured with tensed fingers and tried again to explain it. "Not that he's going to die, but that he's going to do it faster than he expected . . . I can't believe it. I just can't believe this is happening."

"It's terrible," she said. "But what's he got, Gabe? Maybe he can get cured."

Gabe shook his head. "I said that to him, but he – It's cancer and he waited too long. He didn't want to go to a doctor, he said, because he was scared that – He was scared to know." Gabe dropped his head to his knees.

Lightly, Kelsey touched his hair. "I'm sorry," she said. "I'm so sorry."

"He should have told me. My mother should have told me. She must have known. *That's* why she let him have me for the summer, when before she wouldn't even let him see me for a day. That must be why. Because he was going to die, and she figured – like you give a condemned man whatever he wants for his last meal."

"She did it for you too, I bet," Kelsey said.

"Yeah?" His eyes were blazing as he glared at her. "But I was better off not knowing him. Then he could have kicked off, and I wouldn't have cared."

"And now you feel bad."

"Right, you got it. I'm selfish. I don't want to suffer."

"Okay, but if you hadn't gotten to know him, wouldn't you always have wondered what your father was like? Wouldn't you always wish you could have gotten to know him? And how he felt about you and all?"

"No!" Gabe thundered so that she jumped. "I wouldn't have because he was just — just 'A Father' before — not a real person." He cursed and added, "My mother was right about him; he's no good. The only person he thinks about is himself."

"Is that what she said about him?"

Gabe didn't answer. Finally, grudgingly, he said, "She didn't say it. Probably so as not to poison my mind against him. . . . I used to pretend he was some kind of hero and — she never told me he wasn't. She wouldn't say anything about him, just that he'd disappointed her. I don't think he liked babies. I don't think he was interested in having a kid. And now that it's too late — now he has to come along and — " Gabe slapped his hand down so hard on the rough surface of her rock that Kelsey winced in sympathetic pain.

"This morning after he told me," Gabe went on, "I said I thought he was a real — I bad mouthed him."

"Was he mad?"

"I don't know. He said he was sorry I felt that way. Then he didn't talk to me all the way back from Provincetown. . . . I guess he was mad."

"How did he tell you? What did he say?" The only

way Kelsey knew to help Gabe was to encourage him to let it all out.

"It was after we parked the car on the wharf. He wanted to stop for coffee right off, and I wanted to hike around and see the place, and he said he was tired, and I told him he needed to exercise more, that it wasn't healthy to just sit around the way he did all the time. So then he took me to this outdoor cafe, and the table was about two inches square, and all these weird guys were around, and that's where he told me." Gabe shuddered.

"That's awful, Gabe. You must have felt terrible."

"I felt sick, and then I felt like I'd been ripped off." His eyes filled with tears. "How can he die when I just got to know him and — "

"And love him," she finished as his voice broke.

Gabe's mouth twitched as he fought back tears. He turned slightly so that Kelsey couldn't see his face. She reached out her arms, but drew back. He was a boy, and she'd only just started to know him. She waited for a sign that he needed her to touch him.

"Why'd he do this to me?" Gabe asked hoarsely. "Why didn't he just die without sticking me with the job of remembering him?"

"You think that's what he wants?"

"Well, sure. There's nobody else in his life. He told me that I'm his immortality."

"He said that?"

"In just those words."

"But maybe he wants to give you a chance to know

him for *your* sake too. Knowing who your father is — I'd want to know my father, what he's like, I mean, if I hadn't ever lived with him."

"What for?"

"Because, I guess . . . I don't know. To be able to figure out if I was like him at all or . . . even how I wanted to be different if I didn't admire him. But if you didn't know him at all, if you'd never met him — well, if it was me, I'd wonder."

"Maybe," Gabe said grudgingly. "I don't know. Maybe you're right."

The sun-heated rock felt warm under Kelsey's legs. It was a strain to be there experiencing Gabe's suffering, but she didn't think of leaving. She stretched her legs out and began flexing her toes. Water lapped against the rocks; seagulls shrieked and a fishing boat buzzed by in the channel into the harbor — cheerful sounds to contrast with Gabe's misery.

"I'm going home soon, Kelsey," he said at last. "In a couple of days. He thinks he should go back to the hospital and get another chemo treatment or something."

"Maybe you could move in with us," she said. "I'll ask my parents if it's okay."

Gabe smiled and said more normally, "Thanks, but I'd better go back home. There's a lot happening around Albany in the summer. Maybe I can still get that job in the ice-cream parlor. Or if I can't, I'll help out in the park. I have a friend who's a counselor there who said he could always use me."

They sat quietly for a while. "What are you thinking?" Gabe asked.

Kelsey was thinking that she would miss him. She was thinking that she'd never felt as close to a boy as she did to him, but instead of piling the emotion higher, she said lightly, "At least now you know Herb isn't lazy."

She'd meant to make Gabe laugh, and he started to, but his laugh seemed to choke him. This time she did put her arm around him and hold him as best she could.

"Boy," he said when he had himself under control again. "Talk of unloading your troubles on someone. I'm really sorry."

"That's okay. My friends always tell me their troubles. Listening's my best thing – besides swimming."

Now it was his turn to try for a lighter touch. "You sure you're only thirteen? You sure you're not a thirty-year-old shrink in disguise?"

She smiled at him silently.

They walked to the road together. "Listen," he said, "unless he changes his mind and we leave tomorrow, I'll see you, okay? Think I can hitch a ride to the ocean beach with you guys again?"

"Sure. Maybe there'll be some waves."

"Yeah," he said wistfully, "waves would be nice." He squeezed her hand and turned to walk up the hill. She watched him go, feeling bad for him.

Well, she thought, it seemed that her age didn't

matter to him. After all her worrying, he'd slid right by that hang-up. And he hadn't preferred Ria to her, either; Ria wasn't sympatico enough. Kelsey had him all to herself. Wonderful, but she still felt sad for him.

She was under the pines in Aunt Syl's backyard before the full force of what Gabe's leaving would mean struck her. In a couple of days he'd be gone, and she'd be back in the throes of the togetherness summer again, dealing with Mom and Sara and going around feeling hated and hateful all the time. The thought was depressing. It was like being teased with a present that turned out to be for someone else.

11

Sara was sitting on the steps to the deck with her chin resting on her fists. "I've been waiting for you," she said. "Ria said I should tell you I'm sorry."

"For what?"

"Because I wasn't nice to you when you baby-sitted me. I'm sorry, Kelsey."

"No, you weren't nice. You were a pain. It's really rotten, Sara, the way you act sweet as pie around Mom and Dad, but when you're alone with me, you're a pain and – "

"Well, you're not nice to me!" Sara interrupted.

Ignoring the protest, Kelsey continued earnestly, "—And what I think is that you're so bratty to me because *you don't like* me. Why don't you like me, Sara?"

"But you don't like me either," Sara said. Her mouth went down. She sniffled, stood, and scooted into the house.

Ria was in the kitchen grating cheddar cheese.

"He's leaving soon, Ria," Kelsey said. She planted her elbows on the counter beside Ria who kept grating.

"Too bad," Ria said. "So did he tell you what was wrong?"

Kelsey nodded. "His father's very sick. He's going to die."

"Yuck," Ria said. "I knew it was something awful. What did you say when he told you?"

"I don't know. I tried to comfort him, but you can't really when something's that bad." She sighed. "I feel so sorry for him, and for his father. Herb's a neat man."

"Umm," Ria said. "Well, there's nothing you can do about it, and probably it's good that Gabe's leaving. I mean, at least you won't have to deal with it."

"But Ria, I really like him a lot."

Ria nodded. "Um hmmm. So how about making the salad for dinner."

"Ria!"

"What?"

"How can you ask me to make salad at a time like this?"

"Well, we have to eat, don't we? And I thought it would be a nice surprise to get supper ready for Mom and Dad. They'll come home tired."

"*You* can make supper. I can't even think about food." Kelsey was appalled by her sister's insensitivity.

"I'll help," came Sara's voice from the living room. "I can make salad, Ria." Sara appeared around the corner of the counter. "And I folded the napkins under the forks just like you said."

"Good, Sara. You're a real little helper." Ria sounded so much like Mom, the schoolteacher, that Kelsey couldn't stand it.

"Yuck," she said. "Goody, goody, and goody to you too."

She turned on her heel and deserted them. Since Ria wouldn't talk to her about Gabe, Kelsey threw herself down on her bed to think about him. Her effort to comfort him hadn't resulted in much. She should have done more. But what is there to say to someone whose father is dying? I'm sorry. I'm sorry. There had to be better words, but she hadn't found them and couldn't think of any even now when she had time. The best she'd had to give him was her sympathy. She hoped he'd felt it, and that it had helped him somehow.

Don't be mean to your father now, Gabe, she wanted to tell him. You'll regret it later if you are. Poor Herb. Not to have anyone at all to love you, that had to be the worst pain. Maybe he *had* been selfish to reach out to his son when it was already too late, but she couldn't blame him. So Gabe was stuck with some suffering he could have done without. *He* wasn't the one who was dying.

She must have dozed off. The aroma of baking macaroni and cheese woke her. She sniffed the air and her stomach growled.

"Kelsey. Come eat dinner with us," Mom said from

the doorway. She was still wearing her summer shirt-waist, but she'd taken off her shoes, and she looked happy. "Your father and I had a successful day."

"He got the job?"

"Well, it's sounding good. Come and let him tell you while we eat."

Mom had a bounce to her walk again as she went to sit down at the table. It occurred to Kelsey that it must be hard on her, too, to have to leave her job and friends in Cincinnati and start over again in a strange place. Not that Mom would show it. She always seemed on top of things, even in a crisis. Kelsey wished she were like that.

She found a bag with the yellow shorts at her place. "Thank you," she said and ran around to kiss both her parents.

"Look what I got." Sara held up a deflated plastic turtle tube.

"Another present?" Kelsey asked disapprovingly.

"Everybody got one today," Dad said. "We're celebrating."

Ria was wearing a new blue terry-cloth sun visor.

"That's nice," Kelsey said without enthusiasm. She sat down thinking that Gabe might never even see her in the shorts now.

". . . not definite yet," Dad was explaining. The grin hadn't been off his face since Kelsey had walked into the room. "But it was a very positive interview, and it's a company I wouldn't mind working for, good future to it, and the Boston area — "

"We'd have to live in an outlying town, of course, because housing is so expensive," Mom chimed in. "But Kay says I shouldn't have any trouble finding a teaching job, and you girls should love it because there's so much going on."

"Umm," Kelsey said, suddenly chilled by the reality of not going back to her friends in Cincinnati in the fall.

"And it was your suggestion, Kelsey. You were the one who got me thinking about making that phone call in the first place," Dad added. He took her hand. "Have I told you what a great kid you are lately?"

Kelsey glanced toward her mother, but Mom's expression was neutral. No way to tell if she agreed. "I'm glad it's working out for you," she said.

There must have been a down note in her voice because Mom asked suspiciously, "Aren't you pleased with the shorts? They're the ones you asked for, right?"

"Sure." Kelsey squirmed in her chair, wishing Mom would just once say something good about her middle daughter.

"Well, what are you looking so glum about then? . . . Because you got just what we promised you, and your sisters got something extra?"

"Oh, Mom! How can you accuse me of anything that mean?"

Shamefaced, her mother admitted, "Well, it *did* occur to me in the store, but those shorts were expensive even on sale."

"If I were as awful as you think, I'd be a terrible person, but I'm not. I'm really not," Kelsey said. "And I think you owe me an apology."

"You do, do you!" Mother's temper showed in the stiffening of her lips. Ria jumped and ran from the room. She hated scenes. "And when did I ever get an apology from you for all the conflict you cause in this family?" Mother asked while Sara watched in wide-eyed fascination.

"You're so unfair," Kelsey cried. "Half the time you think it's my fault, it isn't."

"And what about the other half?" Mother demanded.

"Look." Dad stood up and pumped his hands at them to settle them down. "We're supposed to be celebrating as I think I've said before. Can't you two ladies — "

Mother turned on him indignantly. "And you're supposed to be backing me up. Why aren't you?"

He hesitated, then said, "There are times when I think you're a little hard on Kelsey."

"Me?" Mother was outraged.

Kelsey found she was holding a fork in her hand, but the macaroni was cold and her appetite for it was gone in any case. She put the fork down. Now she had Mom fighting with Dad, and he hated a battle as much as Ria did. Kelsey looked at him sorrowfully. There was no point arguing with Mother when she was mad. All she'd do was dig in. Already, Dad was backing down and looking sheepish as Mother pointed out to him how well everyone in the family cooperated except for Kelsey who had to do things her own way.

"Forget it, Dad. She just hates me," Kelsey said.

"I don't hate you," Mother protested. "Kelsey, you're my child. How could I hate you?"

"I don't know." Kelsey felt out of tune again and very close to tears. She dashed for the front door, unable to bear being the lump in their midst one second more.

This time she was the one who sat on the rocks on the jetty staring at the harbor. She sat until the sun plunked like a red coin into the slot of the horizon, and the sky washed down in a dun gray. The red light that marked the channel entrance at the end of the line of rocks was the only brightness left anywhere until the lights began coming along the opposite shore.

"Kelsey!" Ria's voice. "They sent me to get you. Listen, they understand now. I told them about Gabe."

"I'm not feeling bad about him. I'm feeling bad about me."

"Oh, come on; don't be difficult. Mom's in a better mood. We're all going to play Life."

"And you were mad at me for not doing the salad, weren't you?"

"Well, yeah, I was annoyed, but just for the minute. . . . Come on, don't be a party poop."

"I'll come home," Kelsey said. "But I'm not playing any games. And if Sara says one word about poison ivy, I'll strangle her."

"You won't have to," Ria said. "I'll do it for you."

"You will?" Kelsey felt grateful. Ria was a good sister, maybe a little thick-skinned sometimes, but basically good. "Thanks," Kelsey said.

She looked back over her shoulder and watched the double ribbon of footprints behind them disappear into the dark. "Why is it that I can get along with most anybody in the world except my family, Ria?"

"I don't know."

Kelsey thought about it. "Maybe because it's harder to live together than just to be with someone once in a while," she said finally, answering her own question. "You know what confuses me most?"

"What?"

"I don't know whether to hate *myself* or the rest of you. Do you think it's my fault, Ria?"

"You always ask me questions," Ria protested, "and I don't know any answers. That makes me feel dumb."

"You, Ria? You're my almost perfect sister."

"No, I'm not. You know I'm not. I didn't know what to say to Gabe today, and I bet you did."

Kelsey shook her head, but Ria ignored that and kept talking. "I envy you," she said. "I wish I was as good with people as you are. It's so hard for me to make friends. Do you know that last winter I even kept track of phone calls to see how many more came in for you than for anyone else in the family?"

"You did?"

"You got sixteen in three days and Mom got six

and Dad got . . . I don't remember. But Sara and I tied for two each."

"You're good with the family though."

"That's because I'm the oldest."

"You think that's what it is?"

Ria didn't answer. Hadn't she just said that questions make her feel dumb? They reached the road. "Come on," Ria said. "Let's run."

They ran toward the lights. They ran home to join the rest of the family at the table. Tonight they would play the game of Life, and Mom would probably pretend there'd never been a fight between her and Kelsey. And tomorrow Gabe would go to the beach with them, and that might be the last time that Kelsey would ever see him.

She'd move to Boston and make new friends, starting all over from bare, awkward beginnings. Ria would go on envying her for being so good with people, ignoring that her mother didn't like her and her little sister had no respect for her. And bratty little Sara would go on seeming angelic and getting away with everything.

Run, Kelsey told herself. Run and don't think about tomorrow.

12

It was such a hot, hazy morning that Mom went around shutting windows. She said it was to keep in the cool night air, but Ria complained that she couldn't breathe. Kelsey paid no attention to their arguments about open versus shut windows. She was busy daydreaming about the coming afternoon on the ocean beach with Gabe.

All of a sudden she heard Dad say, "The ocean's the only place we'll get a breeze around here, but we won't find a parking place if we don't leave soon." Everyone scurried off to get ready, except for Dad, who took Sara's new turtle tube outside to inflate, and Kelsey, who stood trying to figure out what she should do.

If she mentioned that she'd promised Gabe a ride, they'd send her off to find him. But even if she did locate his cottage, she couldn't just barge in and tell him to leave his father on what might very well be their last day together, especially since her family was likely to spend the whole day at the ocean to stay cool. Gabe certainly couldn't go for that long.

"Kelsey, aren't you getting ready?" Mom asked as

she began filling the thermos jug with a fruit drink and ice.

"I think I'll just hang out on the deck and sketch the chickadees," Kelsey said. Gabe said he'd come. The best thing was to wait for him. His father could probably drop them off at the ocean beach later.

"What's the matter? Don't you feel well? You love the ocean."

"I'm fine. But I thought we'd be going later."

Mom frowned. "*Why* do you have to be so contrary? It's too hot to sit around here."

"I don't get hot." It was true. Neither hot nor cold bothered Kelsey much.

"Does this have something to do with last night?" Mom asked.

"Well, I asked Gabe if he wanted to go the ocean with us today."

"Oh, so that's it. I thought you might be angry with me."

Kelsey shrugged. She was, but if she stayed home every time she got angry at Mother, she'd never leave the house. "Even Dad said you weren't fair, Mom."

"I know what your father said." Mother took a deep breath. "Kelsey, one of these days you and I are going to sit down and have a long talk together."

"About what?" Kelsey asked quickly.

"About our relationship." Mother's chin lifted proudly. "I'm willing to concede that I may not always give you your due, and maybe sometimes I'm hard on you, but it's not all one way."

Kelsey smiled. "I never said it was."

"All right then," Mom said. "We'll talk, but not in this heat. Maybe you ought to go see if you can find Gabe and tell him we're leaving now."

"I'll just wait for him. I'm sure his father will drop us off. You'll be at Newcomb Hollow, right?"

"Umm." Mom squinted at Kelsey. "You can't invite Gabe into the house if you're here alone. You know that."

"I know." She would sit outside on the deck with him instead.

She took her sketch pad and settled onto Aunt Syl's lounge chair in the shade of the pitch pine. No chickadees came to the feeder but a blue jay claimed possession of it, screeing at her to go away. When she didn't move, the jay grabbed a beakful of seed and fled.

Dad came out through the sliding door. "We're taking a picnic lunch, and we may not come back until late afternoon. You sure you want to wait for him? You could leave a note on the door to meet us at Newcomb Hollow."

"I'll be fine," Kelsey told him. "I'll go for a swim at our beach later if he doesn't come."

Dad left shaking his head.

She almost called to ask him to come back later to pick them up — at one o'clock maybe. But that would mean giving up his parking space in the beach lot and maybe not getting back in. On days like this, cars waited in line for hours to get into the lots. She was still trying to figure a way around the problem when she heard the tires crackling over the crushed shell driveway as they drove away.

Idly, she flipped back through the sketch pad. Gabe's image caught her eye — roughly sketched, but a good likeness of his head with the unmatched eyes and the long straight nose. She played with the shading for a while, then filled in more of the upper torso.

Why, Kelsey wondered, did Mom have to be so nasty? She'd implied that Kelsey couldn't be trusted, that she was only staying home so that she could entertain Gabe in the house and maybe make out with him or something. Mom wouldn't have expected the worst of Ria or even Sara. Then why her middle daughter? Just because Kelsey did things her own way instead of doing what she was told. Just because Mom didn't like her.

Kelsey flipped the page on her pad and wrote, "Why must you be so contrary?" What else had Mom said? That business about not being alone in the house with Gabe. And last night Mom had accused her of being unhappy with the shorts because her sisters got presents too — as if she were jealous of what they got. Kelsey wrote it down. It helped to write things down, like lancing a boil to let out the infection. Mom hadn't apologized either, the way Dad had, about not believing Kelsey hadn't been the one who smoked that day when Sara lied. . . .

Absorbed in her list of grievances, Kelsey imagined Gabe's voice was coming from inside her head when she first heard it.

"They're not home, but the door's open."

His father's voice came next. "Want to leave them a note?"

"I bet they've already left for the ocean beach. It's the only cool place around here today."

"I'll drive you over if you want," Herb said.

"Gabe!" Kelsey called. She jumped to her feet with the sketch pad in hand and stepped around the corner. He was standing at the front door; his father was leaning out his car window. Herb Altman didn't look any more as if he were dying than he had the first time she'd seen him. In fact, he looked healthier now that he had a tan, but she felt shy about talking to him. Despite how he looked, he was now a tragic figure to Kelsey.

"Hi," Gabe said. "I didn't think anybody was home."

"Nobody is but me."

"Where'd they go?"

"Newcomb Hollow. They'll be there all day."

"Really? How come you didn't go with them?" He looked puzzled.

"You said you might be coming." She shrugged.

"Thanks." His smile rewarded her. "You should have gone, but thanks for waiting for me."

"When are you leaving?"

"Today."

"Oh!" She was jolted.

"We're going to drive to Boston tonight, and I'll catch a bus home from there tomorrow, and my father'll – "

"I've got some unexpected business to take care of," Herb interrupted casually. His engaging grin was as bright as ever.

"That's too bad," she said to him. "I mean, I'll miss you both." Herb's use of the vague coverall phrase, "unexpected business," meant he didn't want any open discussion of his illness. That was fine with her.

"Well, now, since you two have connected, what are you going to do?" Herb asked. "Want me to leave you here, or drop you off at the beach?"

Gabe looked at Kelsey questioningly. "Feel like going to the ocean beach with me? Last time. Last chance."

"Sure," she said, glad it had worked out as she'd imagined.

"Your folks won't mind giving Gabe a ride back?" his father asked.

"No problem," Kelsey said.

She was about to run inside and get on her swimsuit when Herb asked if that was a sketch pad she was holding. "Umm," she said, "but it's not much. I'm not very good."

"So you've told me. I'd like to look at it anyway."

She hesitated. But how could she refuse him? Abruptly, she handed over the sketch pad and rushed inside.

When she returned, ready for the beach, Herb asked, "How much for the drawing of Gabe?"

"Nothing," Kelsey said. "I mean, if you want it — it's not very good."

"Not good? You accusing me of having no taste? I

think it's wonderful." The wry twist in Herb's smile made her catch her breath in sympathetic pain.

How stupid could she be, she thought. The quality of her sketch didn't matter. In a few hours all Herb would have would be his memory of Gabe. "Take it then," she said.

Herb handed Gabe the pad and asked him to tear the sheet out. To Kelsey, he said, "Gabe's the neat one. Takes after his mother."

She saw Gabe looking at what she'd written on the page under the drawing he'd handed to his father. Quickly, she reclaimed the pad. She hoped he hadn't understood the list.

On the drive to the ocean beach, Herb tried to convince her that she should accept payment for her work. "I'm just glad that you want it," Kelsey kept saying.

She was so distracted by the discussion that when Gabe asked for her address, she assumed he wanted it so that his father could send her money. "I don't have an address," she said. "We don't live anywhere yet."

"The post office will forward your mail from your old address for a while," Herb said.

Reluctantly, she wrote her Cincinnati address out on a scrap of paper. She could always tear up a check if one came.

They got out of the car before the jam up at the entrance to the Newcomb Hollow parking lot. Solemnly, Herb took her hand and said, "Gabe tells me it was you who set him straight yesterday when he was mad at me." He kissed her cheek. "You're really something, kid. You're beautiful now, and you're going to turn into a dynamite woman."

The praise startled her so much that Herb was in his car and driving away before she'd recovered. Then her eyes filled with tears. She hadn't even wished him luck, and she would never see him again.

"What's the matter?" Gabe asked her.

"Your father. I feel so bad."

"Yeah," Gabe said. "Yeah."

She looked up at him. "Did I really set you straight yesterday?"

He nodded and began walking past the waiting cars into the parking lot. She followed at his heels.

"Dad and I made up last night," Gabe said. "When I cooled down and started thinking, I decided you were right. So – " Gabe's voice trailed off as they passed the girl in the folding chair who checked cars for beach stickers. "He's going back to lie down," Gabe continued. "Everything exhausts him. He's scared that he won't make it to Chicago driving by himself. I told him I'd go with him and fly back, but he claims some friend in Boston'll do that."

Kelsey drew up alongside Gabe and gave his hand a sympathetic squeeze.

"Well, like you said, I got to know him a little," Gabe said. "So now when someone mentions my father, at least I had one I can remember." He took a deep breath and his voice cracked when he said, "But it's such a rotten thing that he's – "

"Yes," she said when he didn't finish, "it is."

They stopped at the broken-off end of the parking

lot above the sand cliff which had been sliced by last winter's storms. Today there were three-foot swells. Gabe pointed down at the beach. "Well, we got waves, and I see your family near the lifeguard stand."

She recognized the striped bedspread. The family was grouped around it, and Sara, clasped around the middle by her turtle tube, was belly down in the wash of surf close by.

"Let's go for a walk alone before we join them, Gabe."

"Don't you want to let them know we're here?"

She didn't particularly.

"I think we should," he said.

She shrugged and followed him down the foot-pocked trail to the beach. At Gabe's greeting, Dad said, "Well, hello there. Come join the party."

"And look who he's brought with him!" Mom said archly, "our wants-to-be-alone artist."

Kelsey cringed and informed her mother, "Gabe came to say good-bye. Today's his last day here."

"Sorry to hear that," Dad said.

"I understand your father's sick, Gabe." Trust Mother to cut right to the quick.

Kelsey saw Gabe brace himself. He drew a breath and said, "My dad's got to go back to the hospital."

"That's terrible," Mother said. "I just want you to know you have our sympathy, and if there's anything we can do to help — "

Gabe muttered something polite.

Ria kept her head down and her arms around her

knees, as far removed as she could get from the conversation about Gabe's father.

Anxious to unhook Gabe from her mother's concern, Kelsey tugged at his arm. "Gabe and I are going for a walk, Mom."

"Kelsey!" her mother rebuked her. "You just got here. Can't you sit down with us for a minute and chat?"

"But – " Kelsey began at the same time that Gabe said, "Sure." He sat down on the edge of the spread. Reluctantly, Kelsey folded herself into position beside him.

Ria was busy sifting sand through her fingers.

"Have you been in for a swim yet, Ria?" Gabe asked.

Kelsey hoped he wasn't going to invite Ria to walk with them, or worse yet, Sara. In fact, where was Sara? Considering the crush she seemed to have on Gabe, she should have come running the instant she spotted him. Kelsey scanned the water's edge but didn't see her little sister, not until she looked further out. Then she saw her in her turtle tube on the crest of a wave about thirty feet from shore.

Kelsey stood up. The tide was going out and Sara was already in over her head. If she slipped from that tube, or if a wave tumbled her — Where was the lifeguard? The stand was empty. Acting on automatic pilot, Kelsey dashed into the surf and raced through the water.

13

Kelsey surfaced and looked around. Sara was just out of reach, paddling ineffectually with her hands. "Kelsey," Sara gasped. Her eyes were huge and her mouth was a perfectly round "o" of terror. Kelsey put her head in the water and swam as hard as she could. In a few strokes, she was at her sister's side.

Immediately, Sara's power of speech returned, "Help, help, I'm drownding," she yelled.

"You're not drowning, Sara. I've got you."

But Sara wrapped her arms around Kelsey's neck, pushing her under. When she'd struggled to the surface, Kelsey said, "Stop that. What's the matter with you?"

"Save me! Save me! I'm drownding."

"You are *not*, but you'll drown me if you don't let go. Lie still and I'll tow you in."

Reluctantly, Sara allowed her arms to be unclamped, but she promptly reclamped them around her turtle's head. Kelsey began to sidestroke shoreward with one arm, pulling Sara along by her suit straps. Even though the waves weren't high, the undertow was powerful, and they made slow progress.

It took a few minutes before Sara and her turtle tube reached the shallows where the family and Gabe were lined up like a welcoming committee.

To Kelsey's amazement, after Sara rolled off onto dry land, she ignored her parents' reaching arms and threw herself at Kelsey. Sara clung, wailing, as if she'd never let go.

"My God!" Mom said. "I didn't even see her going out."

"Good thing you spotted her so fast," Dad said.

"You saved me. You saved me," Sara moaned.

"Oh be quiet," Kelsey snapped, trying to disengage herself. "You weren't even in danger."

"Yes, I was. I was going out and out, and I couldn't turn around, and you came after me." Sara leaned back and looked up at Kelsey adoringly.

Gabe started to laugh.

"What's so funny?" Kelsey wanted to know.

"The expression on your face."

Ria was laughing at her too. Mom said, "Well, you *did* save her, Kelsey. So you might as well accept the credit."

What's the matter with me, Kelsey asked herself. Here she was, being admired by her whole family, actually experiencing her favorite daydream, and what was she feeling? Embarrassment!

Solemnly Sara promised, "I'm never going to tell on you again, Kelsey. And I won't get you in trouble no more either."

"Good," Kelsey said, "I'll hold you to that."

"What do you mean, Sara?" Mom asked. "Have you deliberately gotten Kelsey in trouble?"

"Sometimes," Sara admitted.

Mother's eyebrows went up. She looked at Kelsey. "It seems I may have been misjudging you more than I knew."

Not a bad approach to an apology, Kelsey thought. Not an apology, but pretty close for Mother. That talk Mother said they were going to have was beginning to look more promising. If it were between equals, if it wasn't just Mother telling her most difficult child what was wrong with her, backing Kelsey to the wall, then maybe . . .

"Want to go for that walk now?" Gabe asked her.

"Can I come too?" Sara begged.

"We'll be back," Gabe said. He took Kelsey's hand and started down the beach.

"Sara's such a little actress," Kelsey said.

"Yeah, but she really was scared, and you did save her."

"Oh, big deal."

"Hey, why do you always have to put down what you do?"

Kelsey shrugged. She knew she did it, but she didn't know why.

"You're a good swimmer," Gabe told her. "I figured you were handling the rescue fine, or I'd have gone out to help you. You know that, don't you?"

"I know."

"And now you've got little Sara under your thumb." He grinned. "How about that?"

"Don't worry. She'll weasel her way out from under quick enough."

"Ah, come on, Kelsey. Sara's a cute kid, a little dramatic, but basically cute."

"If you lived with her you wouldn't think so."

"She'll grow up, and you'll like her better."

"Maybe." Kelsey considered. There were times when she did like Sara now – sort of. Like when Sara had offered her First Turtle for comfort, and today. It had touched Kelsey that Sara had thrown her arms around her instead of running to the parents first.

"Are you going to miss me?" Gabe asked unexpectedly.

Kelsey choked up and couldn't answer. Finally she said, "Are you really going to write me?"

"Sure. Will you write me back?"

"I love writing letters."

He smiled. "I figured you would."

She took his hand. "I wish we had the whole summer together."

"Me too. Believe me, I'd a lot rather be here than back in Albany. For one thing, there's no waves in Albany – except on the river." He grinned, but she guessed that he did regret leaving.

"At least, you'll have your mother to talk to when you get home."

"Well . . . she's a good listener, like you, and she understands me, but she *is* still a mother. I mean I can't tell her everything."

"But she respects you, doesn't she?"

He thought about it. "Yeah, she'll ask my opinion

on things and listen when I argue with her. Yeah, we respect each other."

"That's great," Kelsey said. "I wish my mother respected me, but I'm always wrong according to her. If she isn't mocking me, she's criticizing me."

"So why don't you talk to her about it?"

"Oh, I've tried. I've told her and told her, but she doesn't listen. She probably can't hear how mean she sounds. She thinks it's all my fault."

"So that stuff you wrote on the drawing pad was about your mother?"

"Um hmmm."

"You ought to keep that list up. Then hit her with it sometime when she's in a good mood. I bet if she saw how she picks on you documented in black and white — She seems like a reasonable lady."

Kelsey considered. Was her mother reasonable? Dad would say yes. Probably Ria would agree. "But I did write down how she makes me feel. I wrote it in my diary and left it right in the middle of the living room, and would you believe, nobody even *read* it?"

Gabe chuckled. "*Now* you sound like a thirteen-year-old kid."

"I am a thirteen-year-old kid," she protested, but the warmth of his grin dissolved her indignation.

"Anyway," he said, "diary stuff wouldn't have the punch of a factual list like you had on that drawing pad."

Kelsey imagined THE TALK she and her mother would have.

"Read this," she would say and hand Mother the list, pages and pages of the most recent things Mom had clobbered her with. And how would Mother react?

"*I didn't say those things, Kelsey.*"

"*Yes, you did.*"

"*Well, I didn't mean them.*"

"*Oh, yes, you did.*"

"*You think I'm a rotten mother?*"

"*I'm just saying this is how you talk to me and it makes me mad.*"

And then would Mom promise to try and change? The only way to know for sure was to try it. Suddenly, the idea excited Kelsey.

"Hey, Gabe," she said. "I'm supposed to be helping you, not the other way around."

"Turnabout's fair play," he said.

Ahead of them on the beach were five pin-legged sandpipers and an elderly couple tracing the edges of the waves as they were doing.

"Remember when we walked on this beach before?" Kelsey said. But she couldn't bring herself to remind him of the kiss she'd ducked. She didn't quite have the nerve to tell him she was ready for it now.

He touched her hair, and as if he'd been reading her mind, said, "Kelsey, would you panic if I kissed you?"

"Now?" she said, panicking.

"Well, there won't be a better time. I mean, I'm leaving, and who knows when — "

She nodded, closing her eyes. A butterfly touch on

her lips and nothing more. Her eyes shot open. "Is that it?"

"You're only thirteen. What do you expect?"

"A lot," she told him.

The walk back was shorter. Pretty soon she spotted her family.

"Look at them," Gabe said and added wistfully, "boy, you're lucky to have a whole family like that."

She looked. From a distance they did look wonderful, healthy and pleasant — a TV commercial for the American Family. Mom and Dad sat in their beach chairs reading. Ria was stretched out on her stomach, and Sara was stumbling around trying to hit the paddle ball by herself. Kelsey thought of Gabe who only had his mother, plus a dying father he barely knew. What if this were the last time she was ever going to see one of those people around the striped bedspread?

A spasm of pain shook her. She wouldn't be able to stand losing Dad or Ria. It would even be hard to lose Sara, the turtle maniac. And Mom? No matter how bitterly they fought, Mom was still — she was still there with the cold washcloth for a headache, still the driver to parties and after-school events, still the court of final appeal. She was the one whose approval mattered most.

If only Kelsey could join them without messing up the scene! If only she could avoid falling into the same old bad patterns.

She looked at Gabe. He had kissed her. He had

treated her as if she were as mature as he. She'd convinced him to respect her; then why not convince her family?

Dad was no problem. As soon as he had a new job, he'd be easy enough to get along with. And Ria — all Ria wanted was for Kelsey to take property rights seriously. So what if property rights were silly; she could observe them for Ria's sake. Not so impossible, Kelsey promised herself.

As for Sara, maybe pretending she was someone else's sister would help. That would make it easier to be friendly and trusting. Like for starters, right now, Kelsey could offer to play paddle ball with her little sister and encourage her when she missed instead of getting impatient.

None of it would be that hard, Kelsey thought, until she looked at her mother, sitting there under her hat, dibbling her bare white feet in the sand while she read. To bite her tongue and not answer back when Mom zinged her with a remark was more than Kelsey could expect of herself. Eventually, she was bound to explode. Unless Mom changed, too. Unless —

"*Help me,*" Kelsey could tell her, handing her the list of all the hurtful words Mom had used against her. "*I want us to love each other.*"

"What are you thinking?" Gabe asked her finally.

"About whether I really can change anything," she said.

"Do you want to?"

"Yes," she said. "Oh, yes."

"I'll bet you can then."

A flood of hope washed Kelsey's doubts away. Gabe believed in her. "A dynamite woman in the making," his father had called her. And she? Yes, she told herself. She could do it. She'd find a place for herself on her family's side of the window and belong. Instead of being the awful, ugly lump in the middle, she would rise like newly baked dough. She'd make this summer of togetherness a happy one.

"Sara!" Kelsey yelled. "Sara, want me to play paddle ball with you?"